# THE LOST SAINT

## C.W. TASK

First Printing, December 2024
Copyright © 2024 by C.W. Task
All rights reserved.
ISBN-13: 978-1-955102-04-9

Printed in the United States of America

fictionsmithfamily.com

The text type was set in Adobe Caslon Pro

For Sarah, and all parents
who work so hard to make life
magical for their children.

# The Lost Saint

# ONE

WHOEVER NAMED ICELAND WANTED THE COUNTRY all to themselves. Seyðisfjörður, the little village my family was exploring today, was more beautiful than it was hard to pronounce.

And it was hard to pronounce, even with my Society of Time Travelers necklace, which helped me speak and understand every language.

The lowering sun set the clouds ablaze with reds and pinks as we walked through the middle of the town on a road of rainbow-colored bricks that led to a church with a tall steeple. Although, in December, the daylight only lasted about four hours.

"Red, orange, yellow, green, blue, purple. Red, orange…" Petals' voice trailed off in the wind as she had fallen behind the rest of my family. She didn't like to step on cracks, and the path had plenty of places she wouldn't let her feet land.

"C'mon, honey," Mom said, "the market is closing soon!"

"Oh!" Petals shouted. "Do you think they'll have a freeze ray?" She ran up alongside Dad, who was busy making sure my bundled up and wiggly baby brother, Roger, stayed on his shoulders.

Mom laughed, then hugged her arms together for some warmth as another chilly wind gust whipped across all five of us Joneses.

"I think they mostly sell sweaters," I said, pulling up the guidebook. The locally hand knit wool was supposed to be nice and warm, and I really wanted one. "They're called Lopapeysa."

"Can I at least ask if there's a freeze ray part of the store?" Petals asked.

"Why do you need that?" Dad said, raising an eyebrow. "We're already freezing."

"So's I can show it off to Dr. Freeeeedrick," my little sister said with her most innocent smile and rosy cheeks. "Okay, okay, I'll see if they have a ginumbus heat ray too."

"That's better...kind of," Mom said. "How about next time we ask if there is going to be any S.o.T.T. training in Paris or Switzerland...maybe in the summer?"

I pulled back my mitten to check my watch. We had less than an hour before we were supposed to meet up with Dr. Friedrich outside town.

He had invited me to learn some S.o.T.T. lessons and welcomed my family to come along, but he was being secretive about what he wanted to teach me.

Dad's phone chirped. He glanced at it and got a big smile on his face. "My app says it looks like tonight will be perfect to see the northern lights," he said. Roger squirmed and Dad had to grab his little leg before my brother fell backward.

My Dad talked a lot about his list of things he had always wanted to do, and seeing aurora borealis was at the very top. I was happy that the S.o.T.T. was going to give him a free trip to see it.

As the sun began to set, we ducked into a shop just off the rainbow road. Dad crouched so Roger didn't bonk his head on the door frame.

Inside, a strong smell of vanilla hit my nose before I could spot the candle display behind the counter. The man who ran the register gave our family a warm welcome and announced there was a sale going on for the wood carvings in the corner.

Petals immediately disappeared among the shelves of puffin glass sculptures and Dad chased after her while making sure Roger's grabby little hands wouldn't help us find out if there was a *'you break it, you bought it'* store policy.

"This is perfect," Mom said, checking the price on a small wooden reindeer carving. "I'll be able to get some of my Christmas shopping done."

3

My eyes went wide as I found a wall of black and white sweaters. The intricate patterns that ran across the shoulders and front made me wonder how long it took someone to knit them by hand.

If the store clerk wasn't right behind me, I would have leaned over all the sweaters and given them a big hug. Instead, I picked up one and held it to my face. "This is soooooo… much itchier than I thought it would be," I said, voice muffled by the wool, understanding why the guidebook said to wear a long sleeve shirt underneath it.

"Ooh, that is pretty," Mom said, then glanced at the dangling price tag. "Pretty expensive…"

"Maybe I could ask Santa?"

Mom gave a slight chuckle. "We'll see," she said. "Just don't get your hopes up, okay? Not everybody gets what they want come Christmas-time."

I folded the sweater back as Petals complained about a complete lack of freeze or heat rays anywhere.

"Oh, would you look at that?" Mom asked, stepping over to a shelf and picking up a large white teddy bear wearing a red bow. "I used to have something like this. Mr. Grrfuffle Fluff. This guy is a lot bigger than the one I had, though."

"Why don't you get it?" I asked.

Mom shrugged. "I'm a little old for a stuffy, right?" She put it back. "He needs a kid to love on him."

4

My wrist beeped, followed by a static wash. The S.o.T.T. watch Dr. Friedrich had given me also had a radio function, and it sounded like it was about time for my training to begin.

"Dr. F to Chuckles," the faint voice said. "Do you read me, Chuckles? Over."

The shop owner seemed confused. I gave him a little wave and quickly stepped outside to the rainbow road and the cold air.

"Can we please change that call sign?" I asked, holding the watch up to my mouth as my warm breath fogged over the glass. "Over."

"That is a negative, Chuckles," Dr. Friedrich said. "There is a sleigh waiting for you and your family by the church. Tell the driver you are ready to go and he will bring you over...Over."

"We get to take a sleigh ride?" Mom said, stepping out of the shop with a small paper bag. "I've always wanted to do that."

"Can I sit on the horse?" Petals asked as she joined us alongside Roger and Dad, who looked relieved to have survived without any broken items.

"We're on our way," I said, not sure how much S.o.T.T. training I could do with my family here. "Over."

As promised, a red sleigh waited for us at the end of the rainbow road. The bundled up man behind the reins wore a dark brown scarf, fur hat, and goggles.

"Blankets in back," the driver said, his voice muffled by the scarf. He pointed his thumb over his shoulder. "The wind makes it get very cold, very fast."

In the distance, a single howl multiplied into a chorus. *Were those wolves?*

I narrowed my eyes to see better, and realized it wasn't quite a wail, and it was coming from a pack of reindeer in a field beyond the town.

As we piled into the sleigh and pulled the blankets over ourselves, the driver gave a "hi-YAH!" We fell into each other as the horse took off.

My watch crackled to life again. "I paid extra to make sure you arrive at the Tvisöngur on time. Please be aware that you will pass by the local fish factory," Dr. Friedrich said. "Hold your breath as you see fit. Over."

Before I could ask him what he meant by that, the smell of rotten seafood hit me and I wanted to gag.

"Nose plugs are beneath the blankets," the sleigh driver called out, his voice nasally due to a freshly applied clothespin pinching his nostrils together.

As the sun finally disappeared below the horizon, we reached the edge of a forest. There was a small building that looked more like five domes of varying heights, and next to it was a big machine with lights flashing all over the place.

Five men in white lab coats stood near the machine, taking readings from it. One of them walked over to greet us as we arrived.

"Ah, Miss Charlotte!" Dr. Friedrich said, opening his arms wide. But he looked older than I remembered. "So glad you could join me. Well, us."

The four other men turned around.

*Four more Dr. Friedrichs.*

"Wait, what?" I asked. All five of the Dr. Friedrichs were different ages. The youngest one had a #1 embroidered on his sleeve. The oldest seemed like he could have been a great grandpa and had #5 written on his front pocket in black permanent marker.

"We'll explain our 'meeting of the minds' soon enough," Dr. Friedrich #2 said, motioning toward the rest of his selves. "But first, it is almost time for the arrival." He pointed up.

Above, a murky gray light snaked across the sky. *The northern lights.*

"Aurora borealis!" Dad shouted. "Finally! But why isn't it green?"

"Do you want the short or the long explanation?" Dr. Friedrich #3 said, adjusting knobs on the machine.

"I guess whichever one helps me understand why all the pictures don't resemble this," Dad said, pointing skyward. "It's not how I thought it would look."

"Ah, yes," Dr. Friedrich #4 said. "Your eyes have things called rods and cones in them. Cones help you see color, but only when there is a lot of light."

7

"And rods help when it is dark," Dr. Friedrich #2 added, "focusing on black, white, and shades of gray."

"So when it's night, you focus on contrast," I said. "And a camera that takes a picture can capture color better."

"Precisely," Dr. Friedrich #1 said with a smile. "You'll get to sleep through this lesson at the S.o.T.T., I think. But not to fret, Mr. Jones! If the aurora borealis becomes strong enough, your eyes will start to see the splendorous green you've hoped for."

Suddenly, a crackling noise came from the small, five-domed building. A blast of light shot overhead, unfurling like a whip, and the northern lights flared into life, but in an unexpected color.

The world around us was bathed in red from the exploding sky above and the sound intensified.

"This is scary," Petals said, digging her face into Dad's side. "Why would you want to see this?"

"I don't think this is normal, kiddo," Dad said.

"I got it!" Dr. Friedrich #1 said, staring at his monitor. "I've locked on the message!"

"What message?" I asked.

"It's an SOS," Dr. Friedrich #4 said.

"Morse code?" I asked. "Like save our ship?"

"No, Miss Jones," Dr. Friedrich #5 replied. "Save our Santa."

# Two

I WASN'T SURE WHICH WAS THE STRANGEST: FIVE Dr. Friedrichs, the world covered in red light, or that Santa himself was in trouble.

"I'm sorry, what's going on?" Mom asked, stepping out of the sleigh. Except for Roger, she had dealt with the least amount of time travel weirdness in our family so far.

"It appears as though Saint Nicholas is in peril," Dr. Friedrich #1 said, adjusting his circular glasses. "And someone is asking for our help to find him."

"Who is Saint Nicholas?" Petals asked.

"That's Santa Claus, sweetheart," Mom said.

"Why didn't he just say so?" Petals asked. "Oh, is that like how my name is Daisy, but I go by Petals?"

"Kind of," Dad said.

"Saint is a weird first name," Petals said, then held her hands up. "But I'm not 'posed to call people weird. Unless they are. But I'm still not 'posed to."

"Do you think The Order took him?" Dr. Friedrich #1 asked, immediately receiving a shush from his four other selves.

"What's The Order?" I asked.

"Nothing you have to concern yourself with," Dr. Friedrich #3 said.

"Yet," Dr. Friedrich #4 added, earning more shushes. "Hey! It's too early in her timeline." He turned to his youngest self. "And no, none of our evidence points to their involvement."

I scrunched up my nose, trying to think through this. Each of the doctors had those numbers on their lab coats, from 1 through 5. There was definitely an age difference among them.

#5 let out an enormous yawn as though he were the first to reach his bedtime.

"You," I said, pointing at Dr. Friedrich #5. "You know the most about what's going on, don't you?"

The oldest version gave a wide grin. "What makes you say that?"

"Well, this is the fifth time you've lived through this, right?" I asked, stepping up to him.

Dr. Friedrich #5 tapped the side of his head and winked. "True. Probably forgotten more than I'd care to admit by this point. But, yes, that is a very astute observation."

"Okay, so–"

"But an incomplete analysis," he continued. "The Santa mystery is one I've lived with for decades!"

I glanced back at the youngest version of Dr. Friedrich. "How old are you?"

"Forty," Dr. Friedrich #1 said, and pointed to #2.

"Fifty," Dr. Friedrich #2 said as though he were doing class roll call.

"Sixty," said the doctor with mostly silver hair.

"Seventy."

"And eighty," Dr. Friedrich #5 said with a bow and a flourish. "Which means I'm past due for retirement. So I am excited to say that this is the last mission of my time travel career…to uncover the mystery of the lost saint." He hugged his arms for warmth. "But it is colder here than I remembered."

"Then let us get inside the Tvisöngur," Dr. Friedrich #2 said.

"The Tvi—what now?" Dad asked, scratching his head.

I shrugged. Even the language translator around my neck wasn't helping with that word. It must have been the name of something with no English version.

One by one, the doctors walked into the domed hut. Dr. Friedrich #2 waved for us to follow them in. There were five small rooms in the building, each with different ceiling heights.

"What is this place?" Petals asked, but she quickly put her hands in front of her mouth as her voice bounced around all the walls from every direction.

"Echo...o...o...o..." Petals said, giggling. "O...o... doobie-doobie-doo-doo."

"Doo-doo," Roger repeated.

"Okay, okay," I said, smacking my forehead, which made its own echo. "Let's focus...she said to the toddler."

"The Tvisöngur is a special chamber," Dr. Friedrich #4 whispered, "designed for music. The different ceiling heights make the sound waves bounce in ways you aren't used to. Like this."

Dr. Friedrich #2 waved his arms to conduct the others. "And a one, and a two..."

Doctors #2 through #5 all began singing a hauntingly beautiful four-piece harmony while #1 watched with his mouth open. The song made me feel both homesick and as though I was visiting a place I had never been before.

"That was pretty," Petals said, turning to Dr. Friedrich #1. "Why didn't you sing too?"

"I didn't know that was going to happen," he replied.

"You'll be ready next time," #2 said with a wink. "You have ten years to practice."

"I'll send the sheet music," said #4.

#3 hushed everyone, pointing upward. "Listen."

Faint pops and clicks bounced around inside the domes, increasing in volume until they thundered like hundreds of ping-pong balls, dropping all at once…which then shifted into a melody as if someone were playing a song on piano with impossible complexity.

Dr. Friedrich #4 held up his Chrono device and gave everyone a thumbs up as the clicks finally quieted. "The message has been captured."

"What exactly were we hearing?" Dad asked.

"Aurora borealis," Dr. Friedrich #2 said.

"Light can make noise?" I asked.

"Only in a thermal inversion layer," Dr. Friedrich #4 said, focusing on his Chrono's display. "Which is why we set up the listening equipment here. I could go into how Earth's magnetosphere protects us from the solar wind radiation from the sun, but perhaps that science lesson would best be saved for another time."

"I mean, that kind of sounds important to learn about," I said. "Right?"

"Yes, very," Dr. Friedrich #1 said. "Be sure to keep that inquisitive mind of yours sharp for your S.o.T.T. training. Let's gaze upon what's going on above us, shall we?"

We stepped outside to see the dancing light ribbons of aurora borealis return from red to green.

"Woooooow," Roger said.

"Wow is right, buddy boy," Mom said, leaning in close to Dad, who stared wide eyed in amazement.

"Oh my gosh…" Dad said, wiping a tear from his eye.

"But what happened to Santa? Is he up there right now?" Petals asked, tugging on the lab coat of Dr. Friedrich #1.

"Ah, yes, that," #1 said. "We are about to receive two sets of coordinates, I believe. Our machine is working on matching them, but I'm sure the other versions of myself already know the location."

"Too true," #3 said, "but let us not spoil the surprise. While the calculations are made, we should celebrate the other reason we are here. Did you bring your gift?"

I cocked my head to the side. "It's not Christmas yet."

"No, no, not for Christmas," Dr. Friedrich #1 said, pulling a small package out of his lab coat. "I have it right here."

"What's going on?" I asked.

"No idea, kiddo," Dad said, still staring up at the northern lights. "I can't believe I'm finally seeing this…"

Dr. Friedrichs #1 through #4 surrounded the oldest version, who held his hands up.

The eighty-year-old smiled, further creasing the lines around his eyes. "Now, I probably should remember each of these gifts because I gave them to myself throughout my years, but I'll try to act surprised…because I actually might be."

The youngest man stepped forward with a black composition notebook. "At forty, I perfected the theories that led to time travel. Here are my original notes," he said, offering the present. "May this help you recall the fun and excitement of discovery."

"At fifty, you helped save a young boy's life by discovering how to send medicine to the past," Dr. Friedrich #2 said as he presented the fragments of the glass unicorn in a clear, plastic box. "Which led to more men, women, and children receiving advanced care."

"I get to do that?" Dr. Friedrich #1 asked, eyebrows raised.

"Yes," #4 said with a wink. "Lots of spoilers. But you won't tell the S.o.T.T. on yourself."

I smiled at Roger, who gave a drool covered grin back. The rest of my family didn't know what he would go through yet, but my future parents had decided it was best to not inform their past selves about Roger's upcoming struggles. They had said something about not borrowing tomorrow's troubles.

"At sixty, you…well, you remember what happens, but she doesn't," Dr. Friedrich #3 said, nodding at me while he offered a box with a small compass in it.

"Should I cover my ears?" I asked.

The eldest Dr. Friedrich chuckled. "No, my dear," he said, smiling at the navigational tool. "You'll eventually discover the importance of these items as our paths continue to cross."

"At seventy, you write this," Dr. Friedrich #4 said as he handed a sealed envelope to #5. Tears continued to well up in the oldest man's eyes. "You can read that whenever it feels appropriate."

"I'm certain I will," #5 said, placing each of the gifts in the large pockets of his lab coat. "Thank you all. Now, I believe I must be off on my last adventure." The machine beeped and a piece of paper printed out. "It appears our coordinates are ready."

"Is that where Santa went?" Petals asked, running over to the report. "I can help! I can read…mostly!" She squinted hard. "But that's just numbers."

"Where are we going?" I asked. "The North Pole?"

"Oh, goodness no," Dr. Friedrich #5 said. "If Santa's workshop was actually at the North Pole, it would have been discovered a long time ago. No, further north…sometimes."

"Isn't that as north as you can get?" I asked. "What's beyond it?"

"The moon."

# Three

It took a few moments for Mom to stop laughing. "Let me get this straight," she said, pointing to the sky. "Someone sent a message from Santa's... *moon base*. Who? The workshop elves?"

Dr. Friedrich #4 shrugged. "I probably wouldn't call them elves, but it had to come from somewhere. Santa is missing and they need the S.o.T.T. to help find him."

"There's nothing but a flag up there," Dad said. "Right?" He raised an eyebrow. "...right?"

All five Dr. Friedrichs looked at him and then at each other and gave knowing looks.

Dad sighed. "Well, I guess if there is time travel, why not have a secret base on the moon too?"

"Wait," I said, tapping my chin. "Is that why I saw Santa's coat with Jeffrey at the S.o.T.T. headquarters? He said Santa was late picking it up, but I wasn't really sure I believed him."

"It's quite possible," Dr. Friedrich #1 said. "But Nicholas is a S.o.T.T. member–"

"*Honorary* member," Dr. Friedrich #2 corrected, holding a finger up. "We like to claim him as one of our own, but he has his own means of time travel that we still don't fully understand. Him owing us a favor could make it a good idea to take on this mission."

"And because Mr. Nicholas needs help," Petals added. "I'd call him Saint, but we're not on a first name basis because I might be on the naughty list this year."

"Well, I'm in," Mom said, putting her hand on my shoulder. "No offense to Susanna, but I'll chaperone this time."

Mom had a good point. Before our last adventure, Susanna Friedrich had promised I would return safely from my trip to Scotland, but she failed to mention there would be an awful lot of wolves and falling off of cliffs.

"Besides, I have some questions I want to ask Santa personally," Mom said. She turned to Dad. "Are you okay watching Petals and Roger until I come back?"

"I don't get to see Santa?" Dad said. "That's not fair."

"You saw the northern lights," Mom said.

"That I did."

"And we kind of need to find him first," I said.

"Can you put in a good word to get me off the naughty list?" Petals asked, then leaned in close and whispered. "And ask for a freeze ray."

"Maybe you should ask for something else," I suggested.

Petals scrunched her eyebrows together, deep in thought. "Ok, I'll have to find a thinking cap. Ooh! I can ask him for one of those!"

Dad sat Roger down on the ground, then knelt down to Petals' level. "Let's just enjoy the northern lights until you two get back."

"So, how do we go to the moon?" I asked. "Could we sneak onto a space shuttle?"

The eldest Dr. Friedrich pulled a sleek Chrono out of his pocket that more resembled a remote control than the big, boxy device I remembered.

"We'll figure out our plan inside," he said, rubbing his arms for warmth. With a click of a button, a shimmering rectangle of light appeared in front of us, hovering in the air just off the ground. He turned and looked at his younger selves. "Oh, now, don't get too jealous. You'll all play with the newest version of our house. Eventually."

Mom followed Dr. Friedrich, but before I could step through, Dad tapped me on the shoulder and took me to the side. "Hey, kiddo," he whispered. "I wanted to give you a heads up. Christmas can be kind of hard for Mom."

19

"Why?"

"She doesn't like to talk about it, but I think meeting Santa might be good for her."

"Okay," I said, then wrapped my arms around Dad. "I'll be careful. Team Jones, right?"

"Team Jones." We did our secret handshake, and I rejoined Mom and the oldest Dr. Friedrich next to the glowing doorway.

"So, how do we open…" Mom began to ask, but Dr. Friedrich stepped into the rectangle of light and disappeared. "Oh. Okay." She waved to the rest of the family, then followed him into thin air.

As I entered, my surroundings changed completely. The cold of Iceland was gone, and I almost bumped into Mom, who was also taking in the change of scenery.

The hallway was more like a path through a greenhouse garden with colorful flowers blooming on either side. A brown wooden house door stood at the end with a digital panel next to it.

"How on earth…" Mom said under her breath.

"Homes sweet homes," Dr. Friedrich said as he placed his hand on the glowing square. "What should we have today? Mansion, cozy cottage, midcentury modern–"

"That one," Mom said quickly. "Wait, you get to design your house by pressing a button?"

Dr. Friedrich smiled and nodded his head.

"Decades ago, when my first home broke apart on Prince Edward Island, I got to start from scratch and invented a holographic interior. Much easier to decorate with light."

He turned the doorknob and swung it open to reveal the entryway of a house with sleek angles and large windows letting in the northern lights.

Mom stepped in, removing her winter jacket, and I followed. "So, none of this is real?"

Dr. Friedrich closed the door behind us. "Oh, parts of it are," he said. "If you see a couch, chair, or table… any furniture is solid. You will not fall through them. But the rest of the house is projected light to make the walls, floors, decorations, and everything else all look quite substantial."

"How long until we get to the moon?" I asked, placing my jacket on a coat rack next to the front door.

"Oh, I should have been clearer, dear Charlotte," Dr. Friedrich said, bowing in an apology. "This house can't travel to space, even if it is far more advanced than the prior versions. Escaping the atmosphere is beyond its capabilities."

"So how do we get there?" Mom asked.

Dr. Friedrich stepped over to the kitchen and picked up an orange from a bowl. "Want one?"

Both Mom and I shook our heads.

"We are going to need a guide," he said, palming the fruit and walking over to the coffee machine

21

sitting on the counter. He pressed a few buttons to start brewing a fresh pot. "Someone familiar with the ins and outs of the Santa machinery."

"Machinery?" I asked, crossing my arms. "He's a real person, right?"

"Saint Nicholas of Myra? Born in the third century. Yes, of course," Dr. Friedrich said, holding out the fruit. "Imagine, if you will, that this orange represents Santa. Jolly man in red, popular around Christmas. You immediately know what you're looking at." He began peeling the rind, releasing a strong citrus smell.

"This is an odd way to explain Santa," Mom said.

"Do bear with me, please," Dr. Friedrich said. "Inside are the slices. Also, a part of the Santa process. Not what you see…but they are what you experience."

He ripped a piece of the orange off. "I realize it would be creepy if I ate this slice, but my point is: the way Santa 'works' is that there are hidden layers. And one of those will be our guide."

He pulled out his remote, tapped a button, and the house lifted off, causing me to reach over and steady myself against the kitchen island. Outside looked like Iceland still, but soon we had taken off directly upward until I could see the curve of the Earth.

The planet beneath us began spinning backward and the sun and moon did their dance, creating a strobe light effect. Mom held her hands over her eyes.

"When are we going?" I asked.

"You'll see," Dr. Friedrich said as the sun stopped in the sky and the house floated back down, this time over a city. Then it looked like we were about to crash down into a mall.

"Look out!" I shouted, rushing over to bury my face in Mom's side, who wrapped her arms around me.

"It's all right, Miss Charlotte," Dr. Friedrich said. "I should have warned you about how this version worked."

The windows revealed a busy shopping center, but everybody's clothes looked different. People wore lots of browns, oranges, and teals.

"I know this place," Mom said. "Eastland Hills Mall."

"Good eye," Dr. Friedrich said. "Now, let's find our guide." He quickly popped the orange slice into his mouth and left the rest of the fruit on the counter.

The coffee machine beeped.

"Are you not going to have some?" Mom asked.

Dr. Friedrich shook his head. "No, I've already had my two cups for today. But thank you for asking."

Mom nudged me and shot me a look at the old scientist as though I could explain how odd he was with a facial expression in return.

"Do follow me, if you would," Dr. Friedrich said, opening the front door.

After we exited the house, I turned back and saw the word SUPPLIES written in bold, black letters above the doorframe.

"Did we just come out of a cleaning closet?" I asked.

"No, no," Dr. Friedrich said. "That wasn't there before, but I disguised it to look like a place nobody would want to enter."

Inside, Christmas music played over speakers as people hustled and bustled about carrying shopping bags.

"Wait a second," Mom said, pointing to a big display where a mall Santa sat for photos in the middle of the food court. Parents and children lined up for their turn. "No…"

"Good eyes, Mrs. Jones," Dr. Friedrich said. "Yes, what might seem like a humble actor–"

"I'm not talking about him, I'm looking at…*her*."

Ahead, a girl wearing a crushed red velvet dress with her brown hair pulled back held a stuffed teddy bear to her chest. When she glanced around, I saw her face…a face that resembled mine.

"Mom?" I asked. "Is that…"

"Yes," she said. "It's me."

# Four

Having spent time with my older self back in Scotland, I kind of understood what Mom was going through, seeing the little girl only thirty feet away. I had to separate the two in my mind and think of the younger version of Mom as Renee, even though I never used her actual name.

"Can I…can I go talk to her…well, me?" Mom asked.

Dr. Friedrich stepped in front of her, blocking the path. "When you were this age, did you meet a time traveler from the future?"

"Ah…no?" Mom said, stopping short. "I think I would remember something like that."

The old man smiled sadly. "Then you don't speak with yourself now."

"What happened, happened," I explained with a slight shrug.

"So, what I'm about to go through," Mom said, "the adult me just watched and did nothing about it?"

Ahead, Renee held her little white bear named Mr. Grrfuffle Fluff tight to her chest. While all the other children waiting in line to meet Santa had their parents with them, she stood by herself, glancing in each direction.

"Were you alone?" I asked, leaning in to Mom's side and taking her hand in mine.

"I was."

"Where was Grandma?"

"Traveling. Working," she said, squeezing my hand. "Somewhere up north, I think."

I didn't have any memories of my grandma because she had passed before I was born. Mom rarely talked about her, and I wish I knew more. I tried to imagine what it would be like if I had been all alone at this age in a mall. I hated feeling lost, having to figure things out on my own. I opened my mouth to say something, but ahead, three boys approached, each towering over Renee.

"Awww, wittle baby still needs her stuffy wuffy?" a boy wearing a plain white shirt asked. "What are you gonna ask the fat man for if you've already got this?"

"Leave me alone," Renee said with a small voice, holding the bear tighter. "That's not nice to call him that. And Santa didn't give me this."

"Well, let's see if he can find another one." The bully reached in and grabbed Mr. Grrfuffle Fluff by the arm, almost yanking him free from the girl's arms.

"No! Don't!" Renee shouted, looking around for someone to help. Nobody seemed to want to get involved.

"Do I really have to go through this again?" Mom asked, turning her head to the side. "It was bad enough the first time."

Something bubbled up inside of me. I couldn't watch this happen. I released Mom's hand and stormed forward. "Hey! You!"

"Charlotte!" Mom called after me, but I was going to be a part of her history, whether she remembered it.

"Leave her alone!" I shouted, stomping toward the trio of bullies. They looked up at me and stopped what they were doing. "I said...wait, that worked?"

Running footsteps clattered on the tile floor behind me, growing louder. I turned to see two mall security officers closing in. The boys were looking wide-eyed at them, not me.

With one last yank, the tallest bully ripped Mr. Grrfuffle Fluff's arm off and threw it on the ground right at my feet.

"Merry Christmas. Baby," he said, then the bullies ran away.

I looked back at Mom, whose jaw clenched and tears formed in the corners of her eyes. My shoulders fell as the guards dashed past us. I stooped down and picked up the stuffed animal's arm and brought it over to Renee, offering it to her. "I'm so sorry that happened."

"Thanks," Renee said, looking at the stuffing she collected from the floor.

She took the arm and held it in place, then used her red sleeve to wipe her face as she turned around and stepped back in line for Santa.

"Hey," I said carefully. "Are you okay?"

Renee's shoulders shrugged, but she kept facing forward. "I don't know why people can be so mean." She sighed, then smoothed over a tuft of fluff half covering one of Mr. Grrfuffle Fluff's eye. "It's almost Christmas."

An idea prickled the back of my mind. What if I could figure out what Mom wanted for Christmas as a little girl and help get that for her today, especially if grandma wasn't around much? "Something to look forward to, right?" I said. "What are you asking Santa for?"

Renee glanced at me. "I'd rather not say." She cocked her head to the side. "Do I know you? You seem familiar. Like one of my cousins."

"That happens a lot," I said with an awkward chuckle. I needed way more S.o.T.T. field training to handle these situations. "Well, I hope you get what you want."

"Thanks," Renee said, stepping back into the line as the next family walked forward. "You too."

I left the girl and slowly headed to Mom. "You never told me this happened."

Mom shrugged, then dabbed at her eyes. "It's not something I like to remember, that's all."

"Why did they do that?" I asked.

"Not all kids live by the '*Be Kind, Help Others, and Make Every Day Count*' family motto, you know."

I nodded as I watched Renee be ushered up to the front of the line by two women dressed in bright green and red outfits, complete with floppy hats and bells that jingled.

The mall Santa waved her forward. We stood just close enough to hear what she was saying.

A photographer tried to get her to stand next to him to pose with Santa, but she shook her head.

"I'm sorry," she said. "No picture today, please."

"But that's what all of this is for—" the photographer began.

"It's okay, Sam," the mall Santa said. "You can take a break if you like."

Sam puffed out his cheeks, shrugged, then walked off to join the line for a nearby food court smoothie shop.

I nodded at Dr. Friedrich. "You were saying he's going to be our guide?"

"I was," Dr. Friedrich said with a smile. "Just watch."

Mall Santa peered over his circular glasses that were probably only there as part of a costume.

29

His white, bushy beard didn't match his dark eyebrows, and his suit wasn't filled out in the middle the way one might expect.

"May I?" the man asked, holding his hands out carefully for Mr. Grrfuffle Fluff. "Renee, is it?"

"How did you know?"

"It's my job." He tapped his temple with a gloved finger.

Renee offered both parts of her beloved stuffy for Santa to take. "Please be careful with him," she said. "He's had a tough day."

"That's very thoughtful of you, Miss Renee," mall Santa said, reaching a hand into his pocket and pulling out a needle and a spool. "You'll go a long way thinking of others like that. But you've had a tough day too. I hope you don't mind if I use red thread to sew him up. It comes in handy for suit repairs, but it's all I have on me."

Renee shook her head. "That's fine, thank you."

"Of course," he said, squinting one eye and threading the needle. "Now, what do you want for Christmas?"

"I'd like Mr. Grrfuffle Fluff fixed, please," she said.

Mall Santa pressed his lips tightly together as he began reattaching the white bear's arm. "You're about to have that in three minutes," he said. "Two, if I'm half as nimble as I think I am. But what about for Christmas itself?"

Renee paused, then looked down at her shoes.

"Go ahead, Miss Renee," mall Santa said. "Ask away."

"Okay…I want my mom home for Christmas."

Mall Santa stopped pulling the needle. "Hmm."

"But if that's not possible," Renee said quickly, "maybe a locket, so I can put a picture of us in it so I'll be with her when she's gone."

He finished up Mr. Grrfuffle Fluff's last stitches and handed the repaired stuffy back to her. "We'll see what's doable."

"Thank you," she said, squeezing the bear tight. "But don't you need my address? We moved recently."

The man grinned. "I wouldn't be Santa if I didn't already know that, now would I?"

Sam returned with an orange smoothie, then checked his watch as he stood behind the camera. "Wrap it up, Otto."

Mall Santa lifted his eyebrows. "Sam, you might wind up on the naughty list."

"Sorry…*Santa.*"

I looked up at Dr. Friedrich. "Did he just say Otto? Like the mailman, Otto?"

"I was asking a mailman?" Mom asked, folding her arms. "No wonder I didn't get what I wanted."

"He isn't one yet," Dr. Friedrich said. "At this point in time, Otto is still in the Santa Corps. And he's our ticket to the moon."

# FIVE

We waited until Renee had left before we joined the line to see Otto. I felt awful for Mom, and it made me wonder what other kinds of things like this happened that she had never told me about.

Before long, it was our turn.

"We won't be needing a photograph," Dr. Friedrich said, pulling off a couple of dollar bills from a roll of cash and handing them over.

Sam lifted an eyebrow. "What's this?" he asked, fanning the brightly colored paper money I didn't recognize. "You get this from a board game?"

"Oh," Dr. Friedrich said, then chuckled as he patted the rest of his pockets. "I'm afraid that's all I have on me. But that should be quite valuable in about fifty or sixty years." He leaned in and whispered. "Don't show it to the government, though."

"Why did I even bother coming in today?" Sam said, taking another sip of his smoothie.

I glanced both ways to make sure there were no children close enough to hear me. "We need your help," I said to Otto. "Santa is missing."

Otto gave a big, but slightly nervous, laugh. "Ho ho ho, well...how can I be missing if I am Santa?"

"Show him your badge, Charlotte," Dr. Friedrich said, nudging me.

"Badge?" Otto asked, cocking his head to the side.

I lifted up the collar of my jacket to reveal my S.o.T.T. badge of the sideways hourglass and the motto surrounding it.

"Recruiting younger and younger, I see," Otto said, leaning back into his seat. "But the Santa Corps and the S.o.T.T. have an agreement about...you know." He patted an ornate looking metal belt buckle.

I lowered my voice to a whisper. "We got a message from the moon–"

"Nicholas can't be missing," Otto whispered. "I file my reports every night and he messages back that he received them."

"In the future," Dr. Friedrich said. "About thirty years ahead."

"If we could get there, we would," I said. "But we need your help. Saint Nick needs your help."

Otto's eyes fixed on something over my shoulder. The line of people wanting a picture with Santa had grown long. "I have a job to do here. Christmas is only a few days away and I can't miss that," he said. "If you're really S.o.T.T., then come back on December 26th."

"Fair enough," Dr. Friedrich said, pointing behind us. "We'll just be on the other side of that supply closet that wasn't there earlier today."

"By the way, thank you for fixing my toy," Mom said. "I needed a friend."

Otto lifted his bushy, dark eyebrows. "That was you," he said, nodding in the direction of where the little girl had walked off.

She gave a half-smile. "I did finally get over the fact that my mom didn't make it home in time for Christmas," she said. "It was a lot to ask."

Otto took a deep breath, then let it out slowly. "I'm sorry, ma'am," he said. "The tough requests are up to the big guy, you know?"

"It's all right," Mom said, folding her hands in front of herself. "I mean, it's not...but, you could maybe make it up to me by helping us out here. That would be really appreciated."

Otto nodded to himself. "Oh, I'm forgetting my duty," he said. "Miss Charlotte, what would you like for Christmas?"

I scrunched my nose. "But I haven't been born yet here."

The man in the Santa suit shrugged. "It's still my job to report what every child who comes up here wants," he said with a smile. "And maybe it can be a finder's fee for when we track down the boss?"

I opened my mouth, about to say any of the number of things I wanted, but none of it felt right. "I…will have to think about it. Just not coal."

"Seems doable," Otto said with a wave.

We walked off of the stage so the next kid could have his turn.

"I believe that went swimmingly," Dr. Friedrich said as we made our way to the newly created supplies' closet door.

"Why didn't we ask mailman Otto when he was older?" I said, glancing over my shoulder. "He knows us and would have helped right away."

"*That* Otto gave up his Santa key code when he changed careers," Dr. Friedrich said.

"Why would he want to give up working with Santa?" I asked.

"I'm afraid only he could tell you that," Dr. Friedrich said. "I mustn't speak out of turn. And, please, don't mention his future to him. Spoilers and all that."

We entered the door and shut it behind us once we were all in the greenhouse area.

"Can someone explain to me what you're talking about with the Santa Corps and that our neighborhood mailman worked for Santa?" Mom asked.

Dr. Friedrich pulled up his sleek Chrono and pressed a few buttons. "It's probably best he do that himself."

The clock on the wall spun forward, then stopped as quickly as it had started. The display beside it read December 26.

The door opened. Otto stepped inside wearing a much better fitting red and white Santa suit that looked more like an official uniform than a costume. He rubbed his face, then took in his surroundings with a yawn. "Usually this is the beginning of a months-long vacation, but if the big man is missing, I'm not going to be the one who said no to helping him." He pointed at Mom. "You got your locket, right?"

Mom's eyes widened. "How did you know?"

"I delivered it," Otto said with a wink. "Your neighborhood is in my assigned district."

"Wait a minute," I said, folding my arms across my chest. "The real Santa doesn't deliver the gifts?"

Otto laughed to himself. "That's a pretty tall order for one man." He put his hands out in front of himself. "Now…important deliveries he likes to do himself, but it takes a small army of us to listen to the kids at malls and other places and fulfill those requests." He patted the belt buckle, drawing my eyes to it. "Even with my time looper, it's months of delivering everything on Christmas."

"So you're saying your job is to take wishlists, pick up the packages, and make all the deliveries to an area…" I asked.

"And there's only a small window of time for me to drop them off, so after sixty minutes, I hit this," Otto said, pointing to the circular button on his belt. "So a single night is me revisiting the same hour for months and months, making sure everything gets delivered."

"Makes sense. I guess that's how all the milk and cookies get eaten," I said, cocking my head to the side in thought. "I couldn't understand how one guy could survive that much sugar and dairy." I tried to imagine hundreds of Ottos all swarming over a neighborhood in the middle of the night at once, delivering presents and devouring treats.

"Yes, well...we do burn a lot of energy." He blinked his eyes several times. "I could use some coffee if you have some."

"Fresh pot is waiting. Just for you," Dr. Friedrich said. "Now, how do we get to the moon?" he asked, rubbing his hands together. "I've always wanted to go."

"From the North Pole, of course," Otto said, shuffling over to the counter and picking up a coffee mug. "There's a relay from there to the base, but only for a small window of time." He poured the coffee, took a deep inhale, then downed the steaming liquid all at once without so much as a wince. "Ah, better. Now, I've never used the teleporter, but if it's an emergency, I have the code that can get you there."

"Thank you for your help," I said. I nodded to Dr. Friedrich, who punched buttons on his Chrono to send the house back into the future...well, my present. A display of a map next to the clock showed where we were.

"Might want to bundle up," Dr. Friedrich said, walking over to a closet filled with cold weather jackets and handing them out to us.

We bundled up and headed outside, immediately met by a blast of cold air. The house had landed directly in front of the North Pole. A small, snow-dusted brass statue of Santa stood in front of us, pointing up to the night sky.

Above, the moon hung full and bright.

Otto walked up holding a device I wasn't familiar with up to the statue. "This should do the trick."

Something clicked, then beeped. A blue, circular portal opened up, looking very similar to the one I had worked with back in Scotland.

On the other side was the moon.

# Six

I wasn't certain how we were supposed to survive on the moon without space suits, but the portal led to some sort of metallic hallway. My heart raced. This was not how I thought the day was going to go.

"Is it…is it safe?" I asked.

"Pretty sure," Otto said.

"I think this is one of those times where you need to be all the way sure," Mom said.

Otto shrugged. "I mean, I didn't exactly study this part of the Santa handbook because I never figured I'd wind up here." He gave a dry chuckle. "But I have to figure if something was wrong, there would have at least been an 'out of order' sign hanging around the statue or something."

Dr. Friedrich held up his Chrono to the swirling blue light, tapped a few buttons, then looked at the device's display. "It's safe. Pressure and oxygen levels are normal. No suits needed," he said with a smile.

"But we are going to need to be in and out within about twenty minutes before the moon moves too far away and the link with the North Pole is broken."

"All right," I said, "just a quick jump to space and back." I wasn't sure if that would be nearly enough time to find any clues for Santa missing, but this is what we had to work with.

So I stepped through the swirling portal.

As soon as I crossed to the other side, my leg felt funny, almost like it was floating. I tried to push my foot down faster, which caused me to lose my balance and fall forward.

"Whoa!" I shouted, my voice bouncing off the walls. I put my arms out in front of myself to stop from landing too hard on the metal floor. But since I was moving in slow motion, I had plenty of time to land softly on my palms.

As chilly as the North Pole was, I appreciated that the winter coat I wore helped fight the chill of the even colder hallway. I picked myself back up and glanced above at the circular windows where tiny dots of light poked through the black of space.

*Stars!*

I stepped out of the way as Mom arrived next. Reaching out, I wanted to make sure she didn't fall on her face like I did.

When we touched, static electricity zapped us both with a loud pop. I pulled my hand back quickly, shaking the numbness out of it.

"Are you okay?" Mom asked, now through the portal. She patted my shoulder, and that jolted me again.

"Ow!"

"Sorry!" Mom carefully stepped around me, holding her hands up. "What's going on here?"

Dr. Friedrich entered next. As soon as he was through, he gave a huge grin. "Ah, lovely. This lower gravity will be most kind to my joints."

Otto was the last to make it to the moon base. "All right, everybody good?"

"Yes, quite," Dr. Friedrich said. He put his hand on Otto's shoulder and the static shocked him before I could warn him. He laughed. "Oh, how silly of me. It would be best if we didn't touch each other while here."

"Why are we zapping each other?" I asked.

Dr. Friedrich gracefully bounded toward the door at the end of the hall. "We have little time, so I'll explain as we go."

Mom, Otto, and I started running after the eighty-year-old man, which was more low-gravity leaping.

It oddly reminded me of dreams I'd had when I tried to fly, but couldn't.

Dr. Friedrich pointed up at the circular windows out to space. "It looks as though we are at the bottom of a crater. A clever place for a secret base, but also one that gets hit by the solar winds from the sun." He held up a finger. "Fun fact: ions are a thousand times heavier than electrons and the moon isn't guarded by a magnetosphere like earth."

As we reached the end of the hallway, a metal door automatically lifted and steam hissed out from the top, surprising me.

Warmth flooded in from the room ahead. Looking back, I wondered if anyone else would randomly come across the portal and really hoped we wouldn't run into a polar bear on our way out.

We entered an area that looked far more inviting. Gone were the stark and unwelcoming metal walls. Here were wooden panels and cozy knit things all around.

It was as though someone had moved a little log cabin to the moon, and then expanded it to the size of a cavern.

Red, white, and green decorated the room. Trinkets from all over the world sat on shelves as a fake fire glowed in a real fireplace. In the distance, faint mechanical whirs rhythmically pulsed.

"How did all of this get here?" Mom asked, walking across the creaky wooden floorboards. She stopped at one of the large windows.

I followed, careful not to bump into her. Beyond the window, machines built toys as far as the eye could see. Platforms that looked like moving sidewalks whisked items from station to station so they could be assembled and boxed, ready to go to someone on the nice list.

"Where are the elves?" I asked, my breath fogging the glass. "Or...*anybody*?"

"Somebody had to have sent that message," Mom said.

"This makes zero sense," Otto said, looking around. "The machines need to be taken care of in case one of them breaks. There should at least be a maintenance crew somewhere. Santa isn't known for being a fan of modern technology."

"I think this is more than modern," Mom said, cupping her hands over her eyes as she leaned onto the glass. "I've never seen anything like this before."

"Keen eye!" Dr. Friedrich said, joining us at the window. "By the look of it, most of this machinery hasn't been invented yet. In fact, I'm pretty sure I might have a patent on a hydraulic arm or two being used for some of the more fine motor assemblies being put together."

"Brought back to the moon from the future," I said. "I guess that makes sense... but wait, you said Nicholas was born in the third century."

Dr. Friedrich lit up. "Excellent memory! March 15, 270, according to the records. Well beyond the reach of the Society."

"Then how did he get this far forward in time?" Mom asked, moving over to inspect a bowl of dusty peppermints on the desk.

Otto tried looking very interested in a photo of a reindeer hanging in a frame on the wall. He glanced at the rest of us as we stared at him. "Don't ask me! He's very secretive about it. The only instruction I got was how to use my time looper to make deliveries."

A very faint whoosh and 'pop' sound echoed in the distance, barely louder than the churning of the machines. I closed my eyes to listen for it again. *Whoosh. Pop.* "Did anybody else hear that?"

Dr. Friedrich adjusted his hearing aid. "You'll have to excuse me. My ears aren't the sharpest."

*Whoosh. Pop.*

Mom pointed upward. "I heard it," she said, looking around, then bending over to glance below the desk. "No idea what it is, though."

I narrowed my eyes, trying to focus on any movement in the factory that seemed out of place. I walked along the edge of the room until my foot squished something on the plush carpet.

I reached down and picked up a popped red balloon. "What on earth?" I looked farther down the path. "Well, what on…moon?"

More expired balloons made a trail that led off to another part of the base.

"I think someone wants us to find them."

## SEVEN

"THIS IS AN ODD WAY TO GET SOMEONE TO FOLLOW you," Mom said, picking up the remains of a blue balloon. "Who cleans up this mess?"

"If there's only one person here, they had to have sent the message," I said, walking along the trail.

"And the sooner we find out who it is and what is going on, the more time we have to get back before that portal closes," Dr. Friedrich said, glancing at his watch.

"How long would we be stranded?" Mom asked.

"I would have to pull up my celestial charts," Dr. Friedrich said, "but anywhere from a day to several months since I can't summon my home up here."

"Yeah, hurrying would be good," I said.

The balloon trail led down a hall lined with oil paintings of different men and women wearing the red and white Santa suits. Across the top on both sides were big brass letters that read, "Employee of the Year."

"Otto, are you up here somewhere?" I asked as we walked too quickly to see the names and details on the little plaques beneath the frames.

"Me? Oh, no," He said with a brief laugh. "I'm good at my job, but there are so many who do what I do. Maybe someday."

I wondered what would make Otto give up on being a Santa and become a mailman, but at this point in his life, he wouldn't know.

We stopped at a large wooden door. I knocked three times, but nobody answered. Thankfully, the handle turned when I tried it and the door swung open.

The room we entered was a home library with an enormous mahogany desk and a pile of pillows and blankets off in the far corner.

"Would you look at that," Otto said under his breath as he stared up at two enormous TV screens. They cast a blue light on his face as he read.

I walked over to see what he was talking about.

The nice and naughty lists, one per screen, scrolled through names, home addresses, and what that person had asked for that year. On the far right side was a space for which local Santa helper had gathered the report.

"Oh, wow," I said as lines of information flashed before my eyes.

"That's where my name would go," Otto said, tapping the column.

The whooshing started once more, only this time from nearby. It got louder and louder until it made the big 'pop' sound that made me jump.

"It's coming from the pillows and blankets," Mom said, pointing at the corner of the room.

What I had thought might have been a comfy place to lie down was a tall pillow fort...and there was someone, or something, within.

"Who's there?" I called out.

"You have to say 'knock, knock' first," a small, muffled voice said.

I glanced at Mom and she shrugged. I was used to the corny jokes Dad would come up with, so I felt like an expert in this area.

"Uh...knock, knock?" I said, trying to think of a joke to follow up with.

"Who's there?" the voice asked. "Wait, that doesn't work because you don't know."

"Wait, that doesn't work because you don't know... *who?*"

"That's a brilliant question!"

The blankets and pillows shifted. I jumped back and bumped into Mom, shocking us both again.

Out stepped a boy...no, not a boy. He was made of metal. A boy-like machine wearing clothes?

"Hello?" I said, waving.

The circular robotic eyes flashed over to me. Then his mechanical shoulders slumped. "Oh, you're not Nicholas."

47

"Did you send the message?" Dr. Friedrich asked.

"The message...the message! Oh, yes! That was me!" The boy robot said as he bounced up and down. "You got it! I was worried nobody would see it." Then the loud, whooshing sound began again. A balloon formed out of his mouth and blew up to an enormous size, then popped. "I'm sorry, that happens when I get excited...or scared."

"That was you?" I asked.

"Yes, yes, both the message and the sounds were me," the robot said. "Now...where is Nicholas? Have you found him? I miss him so much and I'm afraid this will all fall apart without him."

"We were hoping you would have a clue," Dr. Friedrich said. "But we have to go quite soon. Any information you have that could point us in the right direction would be most helpful."

"Clues, I have," the robot said. "Ideas, I don't." He walked over to the large desk and pointed to the open notebook sitting in the middle.

I peered over Santa's to-do list. He had every item on it crossed out, except for the last one.

*One more delivery.*

I shook my head. What was that supposed to mean? "Is Santa retiring?" I asked, waving Mom over.

"That sounds pretty final," Mom said, picking up the book. "Maybe he means just for this Christmas?"

"So you see why I'm worried," the robot said.

48

"Wait, what do we call you?" I asked.

"I don't know," the robot said, turning his head back to look at me. "I don't remember. My memory says I love candy canes, balloons, and cream soda...not that I can drink it, and doing so would destroy my circuits, but I like the *idea* of cream soda. It sounds nice. And creamy. Never let me try to drink some, no matter how much I beg you. It would be bad. Sparks everywhere."

"How about we call you Soda Pop?" I asked. "Since you pop balloons too? Or maybe S.P. for short?"

"Espee...I love the sound of that. *Espee, Espee, Espee!* I've always wanted a name!" He spun in a circle.

"Let's get back on task, if we can," Otto said. "Did someone take Santa?"

"Alarms would have gone off," Espee said, stopping his spin. "We had some terrible solar flares hit the moon. He went out to inspect the reindeer–"

"There are reindeer here?" Mom asked.

Espee gave a little chuckle that moved his metal torso up and down. "The animal species you call reindeer, *rangifer tarandus*, could not survive the vacuum of space travel between the moon and the earth," he said. "That's not the kind we have here."

"Alien reindeer," I muttered. "Petals would love to hear about that."

"Not quite alien," Otto said, pointing to a nearby screen. "Show them."

Espee walked up to a small screen next to the nice and naughty list, then used his metal fingers to type something on the keyboard beneath it. The naughty list had changed to security camera footage of nine large space shuttles in a bay somewhere else on the base.

"Behold, the 'reindeer,'" Otto said. "They are the toy shippers that go to the warehouses and then we make our deliveries."

"Why are they all here, then?" I asked. "Does this mean Christmas isn't happening?"

"Oh, no, no, no," the robot boy said. "This year's toys have been delivered to Earth already. The machines are working on building next year's toys."

"Christmas is a well-oiled machine," Otto said, squinting at the screen. "I hate to say it, but even without the big man running things, it would keep going for a long while. Decades, at least."

"But that doesn't mean we shouldn't still try to find him," I said.

"Of course," Otto replied.

Espee typed in a command. The footage wobbled. "See? Here," Espee said, walking over on his stubby metal legs to point to the corner of the screen. "I rewound it to the last time I saw Santa."

On the recording, an older, white-bearded man walked up to check out one of the 'reindeer' shuttles. *Donner*, the label read in big, bold letters.

I couldn't believe I was looking at Santa Claus. For all the nights when I was little, where I wanted to stay up and catch a peek at him, I never found him.

Then the screen fuzzed over.

When the picture returned, Santa was just...*gone*.

## Eight

First off, I couldn't believe I had seen the real Santa Claus on the screen. While it would have been better to see him in person, even spotting him was amazing.

Second, I really hoped he was okay. Just zapping away didn't appear it would have been good for him... or anybody.

"Most curious," Dr. Friedrich said, rubbing his chin.

"Maybe it was a portal, like the one we came through from the North Pole," I said with a shrug.

"How much time do we have left until we're stuck here?" Mom asked, looking around the room.

Otto lifted his watch. "About twelve minutes." He looked down at Espee. "How do we find the reindeer shuttles from here?"

"Top level," Espee said, pointing up with a short mechanical arm. "Main launch bay. Follow me!" His little legs clanked forward and we all soon realized he wasn't the fastest of robots.

"Ah, sorry, Espee," Mom said. "Could you maybe just give directions? As much as I love the moon, I'd hate to get stuck here."

Espee pointed down the hallway. "Make a left at the end, go across the catwalk, then up the stairs! You can't miss it!"

We dashed out of Santa's office, following Espee's instructions. Otto threw open the metal door, which made a heavy bang as it hit the railing for the narrow bridge stretching out before us.

Echoing filled the moon cavern as bright lights shone down on machines as far as the eye could see. The rhythm, if it wasn't so deafeningly loud, was almost hypnotic. I stepped up to the catwalk and leaned over to get a better view—

*Zap.* My arm received a shock as Mom reached out to stop me from getting too close to the edge of the walkway. "Ow!" I said, rubbing away the numbness.

"Sorry, honey," Mom shouted over the noise, shaking her hand. "Just trying to keep you safe. That's a big drop."

"Perhaps we hold things to a brisk walk, yes?" Dr. Friedrich said, slowing his pace. "I regret leaving my cane back at the house." He used the railing to support his weight with each step, giving himself a minor shock every time he moved.

I stole a glance at the cavernous factory where even more machines churned out countless presents. Then I stared at the almost endless machine that was Christmas.

No elves, no humans. Only metal.

Mechanical arms assembled the toys, boxed them, and loaded them into chutes where they were sent off to what I guessed were caves as big as this to be sorted for delivery.

I had never really considered what it took for each Christmas to happen, and the idea of the presents all being stored at the North Pole seemed kind of silly when something like this existed.

Getting a look behind the scenes, nothing felt magical or jolly. Just loud. Something about it didn't sit right in my stomach, and I knew I would need to give it all some thought after we could be sure we wouldn't be stranded on the moon.

"How does—ow—anyone keep track—ow—of all of—ow—this?" Mom asked, tightly gripping the handrail as we crossed the long catwalk.

"Very thorough record keeping," Otto shouted back to us, leading the front of the pack. Evidently, he wasn't too afraid of heights, which made sense for a man who worked on top of roofs.

I held my breath until we finished crossing the bridge and I let out a sigh of relief as the noise from the machines dulled behind me.

Now all I had to worry about was being trapped on the moon.

At the end of the hall was a door with a red stencil of a reindeer painted on it. Otto pulled on the handle and immediately craned his neck upwards.

*Lots and lots of stairs.*

I had almost forgotten Espee had mentioned this followed the catwalk. My heart was already pounding, and from the looks of it, that wouldn't stop anytime soon.

I tried to keep count of how many we had to climb, but after reaching forty-seven, we weren't halfway up. I decided I should focus on breathing and how sore my legs were feeling, even with the low gravity that allowed me to take two steps at a time.

"Go ahead," Dr. Friedrich said breathlessly, waving us along. "I'll catch up."

"Does Santa not like elevators?" Mom asked, glancing at her watch.

"Probably helps him work off the milk and cookies," Otto said.

"I thought…" I said, gasping for air, "you ate those."

"Old habits die hard," Otto said, wiping some sweat from his brow.

Soon, but not as soon as I would have liked, we reached the top of the stairs. On the other side of the door was the reindeer room, which should have been called a launch bay.

Below, nine shiny spaceships sat with stenciled names, all the way from *Rudolph* to *Blitzen*. They resembled spacefaring semi-trucks ready to be hooked up to containers of presents.

The overpowering mechanical smell reminded me of when Dad brought me along to get our family van, Oliver, an oil change. Nothing about that place felt like Christmas, either.

"Hello?" I called out, hoping against hope that Santa somehow still was here. My voice echoed back to me. No such luck.

"Let's see what Santa was checking out before he disappeared," Mom said, leading us down the stairs and to the computer screen across the hangar bay. It had a big blank box and PASSWORD written in bold letters. "Otto? This is your department."

Otto stepped up and typed on the keyboard. It gave a happy little chirp at him as the password was accepted. New information scrolled on the monitor.

"Hmm," he said, keeping his nose inches away from the screen. "It looks like a pretty strong solar wind from the most recent eclipse hit the base."

"Do remember," Dr. Friedrich's out-of-breath voice called from the other side of the room. "The moon doesn't have the magnetosphere protection against the sun that the earth has. There may have been a flare."

"I'm checking the logs," Otto said, typing some more. "Seems like the last thing Santa was looking at was solar energy levels."

"What does that mean?" I asked, having zero idea what the information on the screen meant.

"It means he was trying to catch a wave," Dr. Friedrich said with a slightly out of breath chuckle. "And our search just became much more difficult."

"You're saying Santa went space surfing?" Mom asked, lifting an eyebrow.

"Well, yes and no," Dr. Friedrich said, finally catching up. He put a hand against the *Rudolph* ship to brace himself, only to receive another shock. "The S.o.T.T. knows that he hops through time, which is why we've made him an honorary member. But he's never been willing to share his methods."

The computer beeped again.

"Uh oh," Otto said.

"Good 'uh oh,' or bad 'uh oh?'" I asked.

"Honey, I don't think there's a good 'uh oh,'" Mom said.

"Brace yourselves!" Otto shouted. "Another flare is about to hit us!"

# NINE

"HOW WORRIED SHOULD WE BE?" I ASKED, TRYING to remember back to my science class about how bad a solar flare was. It was something about plasma escaping from the sun, which didn't sound good.

"Usually, not worried at all," Dr. Friedrich said, motioning above. "But here, with no magnetosphere to deflect harmful rays it's a very different story…" He gave a look over to Mom. "I mean, I don't want to scare you, but the speed of light from the sun to the earth gives us roughly eight minutes and twenty seconds…minus the one-point-three seconds it takes to reach the moon first, of course."

"So we need to get back to the North Pole gate before we're hit," I said, imagining how long it would take to return in time. It didn't seem likely.

Otto shook his head. "We don't have eight minutes," he said. "This thing only detects threats as they're approaching. It looks like we have one minute, tops."

"Can we just go into the cave?" I asked. It made sense since the moon got hit with the flares often enough and the factory deeper under the surface was still fine. If it wasn't safe, it also might have explained why people didn't live and work here.

Across the hangar, something dinged, and two elevator doors opened.

Espee stepped into the room, dragging a red velvet bag behind him.

"You made us walk up all of those stairs when we could have just ridden the—" Mom held herself back, puffing out her cheeks. "Sorry, focus. More important things are going on right now. But, seriously?"

"I have magnets on my feet," the robot said. "And the elevator goes fast enough that you all would have hit your heads on the ceiling when it suddenly stopped."

"Seems like a design flaw," Mom said.

I looked around at the reindeer ships in the room. What did the astronauts who landed on the moon do in these situations? Their shuttles probably protected them or else they'd be in big trouble flying through space.

"*Dasher*," I said, running over to the nearest ship and quickly finding the door. "Can we hide in here?"

"Smart thinking, young miss," Dr. Friedrich said. "The ship's shielding should keep us quite safe." He followed me over to the vessel. "And good on you for selecting a more sensible reindeer name. *Rudolph* gets far too much credit, in my humble opinion. The glowing nose is so flashy. I get why he's popular, but—"

The lights went out, then flashed red, bathing us all in emergency lighting as warning sirens began screeching.

"Excuse me, doc," Otto said, keying in a command on a panel by the door. It opened with a whoosh and a metal ramp extended. "Maybe we can discuss reindeer ranking after we get in?"

"Yes, yes, quite," Dr. Friedrich said as he hobbled into the ship.

"I'm coming too!" Espee cried out as his little legs carried him forward as fast as he could go, but the big bag slowed him down.

Otto helped Mom and me climb inside. "Be right back," Otto said. "Guess we're bringing the tin can."

"I heard that!" the robot said.

Outside, the computer beeped, and the screen flashed red with bold letters: *WARNING*. As if we didn't already know there was danger.

"Hurry, Otto!" I shouted.

"I am!" Otto called out. "This thing is surprisingly heavy!" Within a moment, he tossed Espee in, who landed on his side.

"Ow," Espee said.

Then Otto threw the large bag into the compartment and closed the door behind himself with a loud whoosh that made my ears pop like I was in an airplane that had taken off.

"Very good," Dr. Friedrich said with a sigh as he eased into one of the white padded chairs painted pink from the light shining in through the windows. "We should be quite safe in here. No days and days of space sickness for us!"

Just the idea of throwing up in zero gravity and watching it float around made me want to barf—nope, I couldn't even let myself think about that and put my hands over my mouth as a reflex.

I needed to distract myself. I turned to ask Espee a question, but he had already gotten up and tottered over to the controls at the front of *Dasher*.

"What are you doing?" I asked.

"Flying after Santa," the robot said, as though I should have known all along. He pressed a button and *Dasher*'s engines rumbled to life behind us.

"We can't outrun something that moves almost the speed of light!" Mom said.

"That's correct!" Espee said, swiveling his head backward toward Mom. "Santa needs our help, and he's got too much of a lead on us."

"You can't just kidnap all of us," Otto said. "Why on earth would we want to fly out into the solar flare?"

Dr. Friedrich let out a deep *hmmm*, as though he understood what was going on. "That's how he travels, isn't it? He rides at the speed of light."

61

"Is that how the S.o.T.T. does its time travel?" I asked.

The old scientist shrugged. "It's more complicated than that, but yes."

"Well, sticking around here won't give us more answers," I said, especially since the only person at Santa's base who could talk to us wanted to leave. "Are you sure this is safe?" I asked Espee. "Have you done this before?"

The robot gave a little laugh. "Oh, never. Santa wouldn't let me near these things. That's what makes it extra fun, fun, fun!"

With a press of a button, the metal platform beneath *Dasher* rose as the ceiling bay doors slid open above.

"You all might want to buckle in," Espee said. "You know, for safety. Lean back!"

We all decided that sounded really smart and sat in whichever chair was closest. Espee pressed a button and seatbelts shot out from the tops of the chairs and connected automatically to the buckles, criss-crossing like a harness and holding us tight.

"What about you?" Mom asked Espee.

"Magnet boots!" A humming sound from Espee's legs ended with a clank, locking him onto the floor.

*Dasher* launched with a loud whoosh, throwing me back into my seat.

"Where is it?" I asked. "I don't see any solar flare."

"Not visible," Dr. Friedrich said. "Even though it's a billion-ton cloud of electrified gas a million times more powerful than a volcano erupting, only their x-ray and ultraviolet emissions can be–"

Immediately, we were all flung to the side as the flare struck *Dasher*.

Then everything went dark.

# TEN

"Is everyone all right?" Mom asked in the darkness.

Relief washed over me that we hadn't lost each other. I reached out for where I saw her last, felt the sleeve of her jacket, and traced it down to grab her hand. "I'm okay," I said, not sure if I really was. But she was here, and that made all the difference.

*Dasher*'s front display lit up with lines and lines of small green text that scrolled by quickly.

Otto and Dr. Friedrich's faces were bathed in the faint light as they both leaned forward against their harnesses to read the screen.

"My goodness," Dr. Friedrich said. "I don't believe it."

"That doesn't seem possible," Otto muttered.

"What?" I asked, trying to get a better view of the monitor with no luck. "What's going on?"

Dr. Friedrich looked back at me with a wide grin. "My dear Charlotte, this is a list of places and times we can jump to."

I wanted to ask what was so special about that to the man who, as far as I knew, had invented time travel.

"So we're safe?" Mom asked.

Without losing his smile, Dr. Friedrich said, "Goodness, no. Not remotely."

"How did this ship land in 325 AD?" Otto asked, scratching his head. "How far back can the S.o.T.T. go?"

I squeezed Mom's hand, found the latch to unbuckle myself, then stepped forward to get a better look at the screen. I spotted the 325 AD on the scrolling list. "Where is Nicaea?"

"Technically, it is in the country of Turkey, but now it's called İznik," Dr. Friedrich said. "Then, Nicaea was in Bithynia, but the Romans had taken it over by 72 AD. That's funny."

"I'm missing the joke," I said.

"Saint Nicholas of Myra," Otto said, turning in his chair to face me. "Or Saint Nick, as many people know him, was noted in historical records as having attended the Council of Nicaea."

"*Attending* is a very polite way to put it," Dr. Friedrich said.

"Yes, well, they also say he got into a big argument with another bishop named Arius and Nicholas slapped him, getting himself kicked out of the meeting," Otto said.

Mom laughed. "Santa the fighter?"

"That doesn't sound like him," Espee piped in.

"So maybe that's not a list of destinations we can go to," I said, tapping my finger to my chin, "but places this ship has been?"

"*Please navigate to your selected destination.*" A pleasant sounding woman's voice came through the ship's speakers. "*Navigation window closes in fifteen seconds.*"

"So many countdowns," I said, looking over the locations and times. "Let's pick whatever is at the end of the list. Maybe that's where he went."

Otto swiped his finger on the screen. "It keeps going and going."

"I do not believe Santa's last trip would have been logged into our system," Espee said. "Since he didn't use a reindeer."

"What happens if we don't choose a place?" Mom asked.

"*Ten seconds,*" the ship announced.

"Just pick somewhere!" I said.

"Ah, ah, ah," Dr. Friedrich said. "Let's find a time the S.o.T.T. can reach us if we get stuck. We're not getting any help in 325 AD if this ship breaks down and—"

"*Five seconds.*"

The ship rattled. I raced to my seat and fumbled with the seatbelt.

Red lights flashed. I clicked the harness in.

"None of the buttons are working!" Otto shouted, tapping the screen wildly. "Why aren't they working?"

"*Three...two...one...*" the voice said. "*Navigation window closed.*"

All of us were thrown back into our seats, then to the side as *Dasher* skidded off of its path. I slammed against the armrest of my chair, waiting for the roll-ercoaster to finish and once again trying not to think about throwing up in space.

Finally, the spinning stopped.

"I'm going to sound like a broken record," Mom said. "But is everyone all right?"

My chest ached from where the straps had dug in to keep me safe, but keeping me alive was enough reason to not complain about bruises.

We all muttered that we were fine, but I had no clue where or when we were.

I leaned my head back against the padded seat. Above me, the circular window showed nothing but darkness outside. I searched for any spots of light to see if we were still in space. I didn't know many of the constellations, but if I could at least spot the Big Dipper or the North Star, I would feel better.

A green light crept toward the ship, reminding me of aurora borealis. It flowed like water as it neared. Then I realized it wasn't moving slowly...it was just enormous and my brain hadn't worked out how far away it was.

"Hold on!" I shouted as the rush of light swept below and threw *Dasher* up and down, rocking us along.

"It feels like we're on a boat," Mom said as we bobbed up and down. "Anybody wearing a lab coat have a more scientific explanation?"

Dr. Friedrich laughed. "Beats me!"

That wasn't good. This version of Dr. Friedrich had years and years more life experience than the one I was used to seeing, and this was all new to him as well. Maybe that's why he thought it was funny.

I tried to remember what people lost at sea usually did. "Do we have a flare gun to fire off or something?"

"Who would see us?" Mom asked.

"Maybe Santa," Espee said.

"I'll go check in the back of the ship and see if there's some kind of homing beacon," Otto said, unbuckling since we had settled into a slow rocking pattern. "You know, in case one of these things breaks down or gets lost."

Dr. Friedrich followed him out of the main room through a sliding door and they left Mom, Espee, and me by ourselves.

I tapped my fingers on the armrest of the chair. The strangeness of the entire thing was hitting me. First, I had discovered something in my neighborhood that sent me back in time, but it was still just my neighborhood. Then I'd traveled far into the past to another country and met a unicorn. And now I was here, wherever 'here' was, in space on a ship that belonged to Santa.

I shook my head. "I don't understand how Santa is from the third century and has spaceships." I lifted an eyebrow at Espee. "Do you know? You're from the future, aren't you?"

The little robot gave a shrug. "Santa didn't really give me a full explanation of where he was taking me," he said. "I broke down in a mall in 2053, and the next thing I knew, he had saved me from being tossed into a dumpster. But he had me perform a partial memory wipe, so I don't remember all the details."

"Oh, wow," I said. "So you owe him your life."

Espee nodded. "I'm not sure why he left," he whispered. "But I miss him."

"It's okay to feel sad about it," Mom said, putting a hand on Espee's shoulder.

His robot eyes blinked into lines and then returning to their usual circular design. "Did you lose someone too?"

"Hopefully we'll find him for you," Mom said quickly, avoiding the question.

"Maybe we can find who you lost too?"

Before Mom could respond, the door to the back room opened and Otto walked in, triumphantly holding up a small metal box.

"Behold! A tracking beacon!" Dr. Friedrich said. "Perhaps this works like a flare, and another reindeer ship will rescue us."

Otto twisted a knob on the device, and it began blinking. He ducked his head to look out the window at the swirling green sea as we kept bobbing up and down.

Then suddenly, *Dasher* stopped, throwing me forward and light flooded through the windows.

"*You have reached your d-d-d-dest-i-i-in-atioooooon,*" the ship's computer said, faltering.

Outside were...sand dunes? The night sky had been replaced with the light of the rising sun.

"Where...well, when are we?" I asked.

"*B-b-based on the orientation of the s-s-s-s-s-s-s—*"

I smacked the control console.

"*S-stars, we have landed in T-t-t-urkey, July 13, 278 AD...*"

Then the computer died.

# Eleven

"278?" I shouted, throwing my hands in the air in the dark interior of the ship. "How is anyone going to find us back this far?"

Dr. Friedrich took out his Chrono, squinting at the small light it gave off. He shook it several times, then held it to his ear. "No S.o.T.T. members are out there, which isn't surprising." He ran some fingers through his wispy white hair. "Whatever that green light was seems to have moved us beyond the reach of our time traveling comrades."

"So even if we tried to leave a message going into the future for the S.o.T.T. to find, they wouldn't be able to make it back this far?" I asked.

"It would appear not," Dr. Friedrich said. "I am most sorry, Miss Charlotte." He took a long breath in, then slowly let it out. "Not exactly where I had planned to retire...but... No. I'm not quitting."

"The flares are how Santa travels." Otto shrugged. "He calls it light jumping. I'm kind of familiar with his technology," he said, patting the dark buttons that had been lit moments earlier. He turned on his heel and walked to the rear of the ship. "I'll see if I can fix the engine."

"So if Otto can't restart this thing, we need Santa's help to get out of here," Mom said, walking over and putting a hand on my shoulder. "Are you doing okay, honey?"

I nodded, even though I wanted to shake my head. "If Santa went back this way...how do we find him?"

"I might be of assistance," Espee said, opening the red sack he had brought from the moon. He reached in, grabbed the device, then held it out. "I would get worried when Santa would go away, so he gave me a tracker."

I blinked twice. "Why didn't you tell us about that earlier?"

"It wasn't picking up on any kind of signal when you came to visit," the robot boy said. "Which meant Santa had left our time." The box beeped. "And now it is active, so he must be somewhere in the year 278 AD."

"Well, that's a start," Mom said, holding her hand out. Espee handed the device to her.

"So we...walk around until we find him?" I asked.

"Oh, he could be anywhere in the world," Espee

said cheerfully. "This just lets me know if he is alive. It makes me feel better knowing he is."

I smacked my forehead.

"One might assume that if this destination was programmed into his ship," Dr. Friedrich said quickly before I could spin out of control, "Then we shouldn't be too far away from a place he would travel. He could be nearby."

I lifted an eyebrow.

"Hopefully," Dr. Friedrich added.

"I will stay back with Otto," Espee said. "I would suspect Turkish citizens of this time may not be used to seeing a robot. I believe, to borrow a modern term, that they would...freak."

"That's wise," Mom said, then knelt down to get on my level. "Hey, kids have been trying for centuries to find Santa. Nobody said it would be easy." She winked, then handed the Santa tracker to me. "Here. You're better with devices."

The small metal box was heavy and cold to the touch. It had a small antenna sticking out at the top and a little red light that blinked at me every couple of seconds.

"How are we going to blend in?" I asked, motioning at my clothes and then to the town off in the distance. "We'll stick out like sore thumbs there."

"Probably so!" Dr. Friedrich said with a chuckle. "Let me fix that." He held up his Chrono and pressed a few buttons. "As long as this thing keeps a charge, I should be able to adjust our appearances with your necklace. Even down to what we're wearing...but that will drain the battery faster. We should hurry."

Dr. Friedrich turned to the hatch door next to him and pulled on a lever. Warm wind whipped in, taking away the chill of the spaceship. I took off my heavy winter coat, placing it on my chair.

I wondered what would happen if anyone from the city on the horizon spotted *Dasher*. It probably would have wound up in some history book if it was found...or some weird conspiracy theory would have been made about it.

As we stepped outside into the warmth of the desert, Dr. Friedrich's Chrono gave a series of beeps, as did my necklace. Before I knew it, I looked like I was wearing a long, brown robe, even though I still had my regular clothes on.

If it was this warm when the sun was barely up, I didn't look forward to the heat of the day.

"I've never been to Turkey," Mom said as she exited *Dasher*. "Your grandmother went several times, and when she got back from her first trip, I asked her if that's where all the turkeys lived."

I laughed. Mom hadn't told me that story before. She actually hadn't told me many stories about grandma, even though she seemed to have had a really interesting life. "Why was she in Turkey?"

"Researching the chevrotain," Mom said.

"Chevro-what now?" I asked.

"Chevrotain," Dr. Friedrich said. "One of Susanna's favorite animals," Dr. Friedrich said, joining us as we trekked toward the town.

"The smallest hoofed mammal in the world," Mom said, holding a finger in the air. "Some people call it a 'mouse deer.' I call it the reason I didn't see your grandmother for five months." She gave a sad smile. "Her research got me an A+ on a middle-school paper once, but I would have been okay getting a C if it meant spending more time with her."

"I'm sorry," I said, scuffing at the ground with my shoe. It was becoming more apparent why grandma wasn't talked about much.

"It's all right," Mom said. "Some parents have jobs that keep them from seeing their kids." She squeezed my shoulder and smiled. "That's a big reason I wanted to go on this trip. You're going on these adventures, and I want to make sure I get to spend some time with you."

I nodded, wondering if she felt like I was leaving her behind too with my S.o.T.T. missions.

The Santa tracker's light blipped red at a faster rate as we continued onward. "Oh, look," Dr. Friedrich said. "Perhaps that means we're getting closer to Santa."

"So, how do I not stick out?" I asked. "I know my clothes and voice are covered, but I don't want to insult someone by doing something wrong."

"Oh, just leave that to me," Dr. Friedrich said with a smile. "The Turkish people are known for their hospitality and inquisitiveness…and some get Istanbul and Constantinople mixed up, but in fact, the city is called neither of those names at the moment!"

"Isn't there a song about that?" Mom asked.

Dr. Friedrich laughed. "That there is, but they failed to mention it was known as Byzantium until 330 AD."

"I'll remember that for my next history test on the Middle East," I said, paying more attention to how fast the red light blinked. "Assuming I find my way back to a classroom someday."

I swung the antenna on the tracker left, then right. When it wasn't pointed at the city, the light didn't flash quickly. When I aimed it straight ahead, it sped up. "Santa has to be somewhere around here."

Without too much trouble, the three of us walked past the tall marble columns at the city's gates. We drew little attention except for when we needed to scoot out of the way to let wagons pass.

We reached the market square where vendors were setting up their booths to sell their goods for the day and a line was forming at the well in the center. Townspeople with wooden buckets waited patiently for their turns to collect water.

I tried to hide the device so the modern technology wouldn't be noticed, but when nobody was looking, I checked to make sure we were on the right track.

"How's it going?" Mom asked quietly. "Are we getting closer?"

The light was blinking so quickly that I didn't think it could go much faster. "Uh...he might be here," I said. "Does anybody see him?"

Scanning the market square, I couldn't find any portly, jolly fellows with long beards wearing red.

Motion caught my eye from above. A young boy carefully balanced along the roof's edge. Out of curiosity, I pointed the Santa tracker at him.

It stopped blinking and went solid.

"Hey! It's you!" I shouted before thinking.

The boy's eyes opened wide.

Then he slipped.

# Twelve

"Oh, no!" I shouted as the boy fell and slid down the tiled roof. I spotted a wagon filled with hay next to me and pushed it as hard as I could. I didn't think it would make it over in time to save him, but I had to try something.

Mom saw what I was doing and threw her shoulder into the wooden side to boost it into position faster for the boy to land.

But nothing happened.

The kid hung on the edge of the roof, feet dangling as he grunted with an effort to not lose his grip.

"Are you okay?" I called up.

"Uh…no?" the boy said, pulling himself up so his elbow reached above the ledge.

"What are you doing up there?" I asked, unsure of what else to say.

"Trying to not fall…again," he said with a grunt. He hiked a foot up to the roof's edge, but the tiles he hung from broke loose. He dropped ten feet down into the hay, throwing his hands up to defend himself against other roof pieces that decided they wanted to obey gravity and play follow the leader.

Mom and I rushed over to check on him as he struggled to dig himself out of the pile of hay. Donkeys brayed at the inedible intruder.

"You have a cut," I said, pointing above my eyebrow.

He stood up to about my height, then carefully touched his fingers to his olive-complexion forehead, wincing when he felt the wound. "So I do. Ow."

"We should make sure he's not concussed," Mom said.

"What's concussed?" the boy asked.

"Can you tell us your name?" I asked.

"Nicholas."

My eyes shot open wide. "Did you say Nicholas?" I wanted to double check the tracker. We weren't tracking Santa, at least the Santa Claus I was expecting, but we had found the younger version of him.

"…yes?"

"Oh, no," I said.

"Yes, this is quite problematic," Dr. Friedrich said, folding his arms and placing his chin in his hand.

Young Nicholas furrowed his brow at Dr. Friedrich. "What's your name?" he asked me.

"Charlotte."

"I do not think I have ever heard that one before," Nicholas said. "Am I in trouble?"

"Well, no, I don't think so," I said.

"Nicholas!" a large, bearded man shouted from across the courtyard as more merchants began crowding the square. "What are you doing out here?"

"I was on my way to buy breakfast for the other children," he called out.

"Let the orphanage handle its own business!" the man said, jogging toward us.

"I am afraid I must be off," Nicholas said, patting himself all over. "Oh, no...guess I will wind up making someone's day."

"What?" I asked.

"My satchel," he said with a sigh. "Just have to come back and find it later." He turned on his heel and bolted.

"Wait," I said to no effect as he continued to disappear into the crowd. "How is a kid version of Santa supposed to get us home?"

Dr. Friedrich made a shooing motion with both hands. "Follow him! We don't have any other leads! I'll track you by your necklace."

I nodded and took off. Mom tried to stick with me, but if I slowed down, I would lose Nicholas down the long city streets that bustled with more and more people now that their daily activities had gotten underway.

Nicholas turned left at the upcoming intersection, and I followed him, almost slamming right into a fruit wagon. I jumped out of the way just in time, but lost sight of his curly mop of dark hair in the crowded alleyway.

Then I spotted movement above.

The boy had scaled the side of the building, returning to his rooftop running ways. I chuckled to myself, imagining how that skill would come in handy for him later in life.

But how was I going to meet that older version of him? As I dodged between two arguing merchants, I wondered what the connection was to this date and why it was in *Dasher*'s navigation computer.

Nicholas nimbly hopped from rooftop to rooftop, then glanced over his shoulder and spotted me. He gave a little wave, then stopped at the spire of a building taller than any of the others nearby. He carefully climbed in through a stone opening that housed a bell, then disappeared inside.

To make sure he hadn't gone out through another window, I jogged past the main entrance. The empty rooftops told me he was still in the building, so I found my way to the front door, out of breath and sweaty.

I pulled on the large circular knocker. The cool air that breezed out as the door opened was a welcome relief. Aside from the sunlight filtering in from the entrance, the only other light came from some candles burning together.

I wanted to call out for Nicholas, but didn't want to break the silence or earn the attention of someone who might chase me away. I pulled out the Santa tracker, which flashed quickly.

He was still nearby.

Taking several careful steps forward, I pointed the device in different directions. Oddly enough, the candles made the light flash faster.

"What are you doing?" a voice said from behind, startling me.

Two shadows filtered in on the stone floors from outside, making me jump.

"There you are," Mom said, catching her breath.

"I couldn't lose him," I whispered, then held up the device. "I'm not sure why he's hiding here."

"Charlotte," Dr. Friedrich said, wiping sweat from his forehead and taking a moment to compose himself. "I have a science quiz for you."

"Right now?" I asked, lifting an eyebrow.

"Yes, it is an excellent opportunity," Dr. Friedrich said, holding a finger up. "Which color flame is hotter: blue or—"

"Blue," I said, instantly knowing the answer. "It's the hottest."

"Oh, let me finish, won't you?" Dr. Friedrich said. "You're just like Susanna. Actually, violet burns the hottest at 3,000 degrees Fahrenheit, but it was not one of the two options. Remember, the heat spectrum follows the color spectrum."

"So red flame is the coolest," Mom said. "But I agree with Charlotte. What's with the quiz?"

"Not every color of the spectrum is connected to its temperature," Dr. Friedrich said, then stepped aside. "For instance, green."

Among the many white candles burning was a single red wax candle with a flickering green flame atop it.

"Where did that come from?" I asked, stepping closer.

"Not 278 AD, one would assume," Dr. Friedrich said, leaning in toward the unique fire. "Fascinating."

I held the device up to the candle to confirm it was setting off the tracker. "Why?"

Then the fire grew, lifting like a northern light trail until it covered the room's ceiling.

"What on earth..." I muttered, then jumped back as a flash of brightness made me blink and jerk away.

Suddenly, the sound of talking filled the room.

I rubbed my eyes. The room was full of people shuffling into their pews.

A man in long robes stood at the end of the rows of benches, raising his arms to gather everyone's attention.

*Did we just jump through time because of the candle?*
I looked over at the red pile of wax. The dying green

light on the wick immediately snuffed out with a wisp of smoke.

Mom and Dr. Friedrich were still with me in the lobby, confusion playing on their faces.

"Incredible," Dr. Friedrich whispered. He stepped over to wax and waved his hand at it a few times, cooling the melted substance until it solidified. Then he pried it off of the platform and dropped it into his pocket. "A little something for later, perhaps."

The front door burst open, letting frigid air inside as a man in a thick fur coat dusted the snow from his shoulders. He almost bowled into me, focused on the pews ahead.

"Whoa," I said, stepping out of the way.

He took off his cap and nodded an apology, then quickly slipped into the last row as the rest of the congregation stood.

"Did we just jump forward in time?" Mom asked, kicking a bit of slush off her shoe. "I don't think snow was in the forecast this morning."

"I hope not," I said.

"Why is that?" Dr. Friedrich asked.

"Because then how would we find Otto, Espee, and *Dasher*?" I asked. "We might be even further away from getting home."

"Maybe we're supposed to be here," Mom said, motioning to the people in the church. "Does the tracker show San…Nicholas is here?"

"Good idea," I said, carefully pulling the small box out. It blinked slowly no matter which way I pointed it. "He exists at this time, but he isn't close."

The wooden pews creaked as dozens of people sat down.

"Maybe we should blend in until we figure out what to do," I said.

I led Mom and Dr. Friedrich to the last bench in the back of the room and slid in next to the man who had nearly run me over. I was about to wave hello when I realized he was leaning forward, hands clasped and pressed against his forehead.

"Almighty God," he whispered. "Please answer my prayers once more. You are the author and provider, and I come to you again asking for a miracle."

I felt bad for listening in and tried to make it not terribly obvious, looking straight ahead. The people in front of us would occasionally look back at the man as a disruption, since nobody else was praying out loud.

"I know you are not one to repeat miracles in the same way," he continued, "but twice now, when my daughters needed a dowry, you provided the money necessary in our stockings. I am of but humble means. I cannot provide for my dear Deniz, and I cannot leave her to a fate unspeakable in a place like this."

I lifted an eyebrow. *A present in a stocking?*

Santa was on the move.

# Thirteen

The man continued to pray. "I come to you in faith that my daughter's heavenly father can provide when I cannot," he said. "Amen."

"Amen," I repeated by habit, then shut my mouth.

He looked at me.

"Ah…amen." I pointed at the priest at the front of the room. "That was good."

He furrowed his brow at me, then stood. "Excuse me." He brushed past me and walked into the lobby.

"Mom, we need to follow him," I whispered.

"Wait, what?" Mom asked.

"Charlotte is right," Dr. Friedrich said, sticking his pinky in his ear and twisting. "I am afraid I was also eavesdropping. It is an unfortunate benefit of hearing aids from time to time."

"Is Nicholas going to help him?" I asked, hopeful.

"It lines up with one of the few origin stories for the jolly man," Dr. Friedrich said, standing and earning some more looks from the crowd. He waved and gave a kind smile. "But we must hurry."

Mom and I followed Dr. Friedrich out into the chilly night. It was a shame that the clothes our necklaces projected over our bodies didn't keep us warm.

The man disappeared around the corner. I started to jog after him, but I slipped on some ice.

"Whoa, there," Mom said, catching my arm and keeping me from bruising my backside. "We don't have to run this time."

I was about to protest, but then I noticed the footprints in the freshly fallen snow. With no one else out and about this evening, the tracks would be far easier to follow than unicorns in Scotland. Nodding, I stepped carefully and kept my eyes locked on the man's path.

"You were saying something about Santa's history," I said, looking to Dr. Friedrich.

He brightened up. "Ah, yes, the story of the three daughters," he said. "Legend has it that Nicholas lost his parents at an early age, so he inherited a large sum of money...which he gave out generously."

"Sounds like him," I said. "So, the guy mentioned a dowry. What's that?"

"Back in these times," Mom said, putting an arm around my shoulder and pulling me in close, "when a daughter was going to marry a man, her father would give a gift in order for the groom's family to accept her. If you didn't have wealth, marrying was difficult."

"And the alternatives were not pleasant," Dr. Friedrich said, "so let's leave it at that. But the story goes that Nicholas left money in the stockings that were hung out to dry."

"So he'll be sneaking into their house tonight?" I asked, imagining the boy jumping from rooftop to rooftop.

"Well, if the events play out as expected," Dr. Friedrich said as they rounded the street corner. "We must have hopped forward in time. Nicholas was the Bishop of Myra in that story."

We continued to follow at a distance, and Mom seemed lost in thought. "You okay?" I asked.

Mom shrugged, then nodded. "Just worried about Petals and Roger."

"And Dad?"

Mom laughed. "Oh, that goes without saying," she said. "I certainly didn't expect to be stuck in time when I woke up this morning."

"We'll find a way out," I said, not sure I could back it up.

"You sound pretty certain," Mom said, nudging me with her elbow.

"I'm two for two on getting unstuck," I said, smiling.

"That's true," Mom said with a nod, "but right now, two out of three is bad."

We left the city's center and made it to a neighbor-hood. The man had reached his house, so we ducked next to a building across the street in case he might look back to spot us.

Then someone's hand landed on my shoulder.

I jumped away in shock, letting out a little yelp.

Mom threw a hard punch at whoever was behind me. "Hands off her!"

The man held his mittens up. "Whoa, whoa, I am very sorry," he said. "I meant no harm. It seems we are of the same mind right now."

As I calmed down, I recognized the boyish glint in the middle-aged man's eyes. It was Nicholas, but not quite the Santa Claus we were after.

He squinted at me. "The girl from the market-place," he said, cocking his head to the side. "But that was…years ago. How is this possible?"

"It's…" I looked over at Dr. Friedrich, who lifted an eyebrow. "…very complicated."

"If I am in the presence of an angel, please let me know," Nicholas said, removing his cap.

I laughed, then covered my mouth. "No, I, uh… are you planning on giving that family some money for a dowry?"

Nicholas's smile disappeared. He reached into his pocket and pulled out a small sack that clinked with coins as he shifted it in his hand. "It would appear my actions have not been as secret as I had hoped."

"The man was praying for a miracle back in the church," I said.

"Yes, two nights now I've delivered a bag like this," Nicholas said, tossing and catching it. "Third night, third daughter. Their father lost everything, so if I can be the hands and feet of the Lord, then I see nothing wrong with him believing in miracles." He knelt down at my level. "May I count on your secrecy?"

I nodded. "Maybe after this, we could ask for your help," I said. "We're…kind of off-course, and we were hoping you might point us in the right direction."

Dr. Friedrich pulled the red wax out of his coat pocket. "Would you know anything about a candle like this yet?"

"Yet?" Nicholas asked, inspecting the waxy lump. He gave a low hum, glancing at me. "I believe things are adding up in my mind."

"So you could help?" I asked, hopeful.

"Perhaps," Nicholas said, offering over the satchel of money to me. "If you deliver this to his house, I will see what I can do to assist you in your travels, Charlotte."

"You remembered my name," I said, accepting the surprisingly heavy bag.

He beamed. "I have an excellent memory."

I poked my head around the corner to spy the home. Through the window, the father hugged his crying daughter while the two sisters also consoled her. I wasn't sure if Nicholas wanted me to experience an early bit of Christmas magic or if he just was avoiding getting caught, but it seemed like a fun task.

"All right," I said. "I'll be back."

"Whoa, whoa, whoa," Mom said. "You're not going into a stranger's house by yourself. I'm coming with you."

"And I shall stay here to have some riveting discussions with Saint Nicholas," Dr. Friedrich said.

"Saint?" Nicholas said with a laugh. "That is taking it far."

Mom and I left them behind and did our best to act casually as we crossed the street in case anyone spotted us.

Passing the house, I noticed there wasn't smoke coming out of the top. The opening in the roof seemed big enough for a girl my size to shimmy down. Yes, I'd get covered in soot, but how could I pass up the full Santa experience?

"I'll do the chimney thing if you can you distract them," I whispered.

"Distract them?"

"Um, maybe go in the backyard and yell something Petals would say?"

"She is a showstopper, isn't she?" Mom said with a soft chuckle. We reached the side of the house next to a large stack of firewood that I could stand on to climb up onto the roof. She took a wide stance and clasped her hands for me to step into. "Here, I'll give you a leg up."

I climbed atop the pile of wood that mercifully didn't shift too much beneath me.

"Be careful going down the chimney," Mom said, then grabbed a log and brought it with her. "I'll see you by the front door, okay?"

"Got it," I grunted as I hauled myself on top of the roof. It wasn't too steep to walk on, but I couldn't go tromping around above the family before Mom's diversion.

I waited, watching the steam from my breath carry away on this wind. How long until Mom—

"Behold!" Mom shouted from behind the house. "I am Sir Log of Loggertown, here to grant you three wishes, but only if you can catch me!"

I held a laugh in as I heard voices below and then the back door opened. This was my chance.

I ran to the chimney and hopped over the edge, pressing my hands and feet against the walls, and scooted down until I reached the small pile of wood at the bottom.

The soot tickled my nose and throat, but I did my best not to cough.

"Who was it, papa?" one daughter said outside.

"The town fool, no doubt," the father said.

I had to hurry. I spotted the stockings hung up above the fireplace, and I slipped the sack of coins in the smallest one, then turned and unlocked the front door.

Mom flung it open, then froze as she looked over my shoulder. "Charlotte."

"What?" I said, turning around to see the red candle with a green flame on top of the mantle. "Wait, wait," I whispered as the light grew taller and brighter.

"Who are you two?" the father shouted as he returned inside.

I spun, putting my hands up. My heart raced as Mom wrapped her arms around me. "I...uh...am a—"

The room filled with green.

Then everything flashed white.

## Fourteen

My surroundings changed yet again as I fell out of the light.

Pressure pushed across my chest like a seatbelt. Something padded my fall, and the restraint let go.

"Ow…" Mom groaned.

"Are you okay?" I said, rolling off of her and finding myself in some tall grass. I parted it and saw her struggling to take a breath.

She gasped, then burst into a laugh. "Let's not do that again."

Another candle, another new location. We were in a field next to a large stone building. It was night; the snow was gone, and thankfully so was the chill. "Sir Log?"

Mom pulled herself up to a seated position. "Petals didn't tell you about Sir Log of Loggertown?" she asked. "A few months ago, when you were in school, Petals had this idea that she wanted a piece of firewood for a pet and named it that…then screamed bloody murder when a centipede crawled out of it. So she decided Sir Log belonged outdoors. She never got within ten feet of it again, but wouldn't let Dad chuck it back into the woods."

"So that's why Dad always mows around that random piece of wood in the yard?" I laughed until tears formed at the corners of my eyes and Mom joined in.

We both needed a laugh.

I may have been lost in time, but at least I wasn't alone.

I hugged Mom and gave her a big squeeze. She returned the embrace, then said, "What was that for?"

"Just glad you're here," I said, standing and offering her my hand. "Now, let's figure out where and when we are."

As I bent over, the metal Santa tracker fell out of my pocket. Mom picked it up and brushed off some dirt. I sighed in relief that it blinked rapidly. When she pointed it at the stone building, it went solid red. "Oh, good," she said. "He's right over there."

Noise and light filtered through an open window, so we walked over and peeked inside.

Several hundred men had gathered around tables, dressed in their best, but it was obvious they all came from different cultures. One man stood across the room wearing what kind of looked like Egyptian robes and waved his arms while he spoke.

"You cannot place the two at the same level!" he yelled. "It is blasphemy!"

A balding, older man roared. "None of this works if the father and the son are not one and the same!"

*Nicholas.*

"What is the point in the Emperor having us all here if we cannot at least come to an agreement on the most foundational building block?" Nicholas shouted, clasping his fingers together and holding both hands out for emphasis.

"Easy, friend," the Egyptian said in a less than friendly tone. "You forget yourself."

"And you forget who he truly is!" Nicholas said, pointing a finger at the ceiling.

"Must we give this overbearing oaf the floor—" the Egyptian began, but was stopped as Nicholas, with surprising speed, stomped over and slapped the man's face.

The assembly broke into shouts. Men rose to separate the two. With everybody on their feet, my vision was obscured.

"I am not proud of that moment," a deep, older voice said from behind me, making me jump right into Mom.

I whirled around. Light from the window cast across a bushy beard and a dark red suit trimmed in white.

This was the version of Santa I had always imagined. I felt my knees grew weak in relief that we had finally found the man we had been looking for.

I tried to speak, but I was in a state of awe.

"You keep doing that!" Mom said, swatting his arm and destroying the moment.

"Please accept my apology, Renee," Santa said.

"For which thing?" Mom said.

"How can you be mad at Santa?" I asked.

"I was a little girl who just wanted my mother on Christmas," Mom said, folding her arms. "That's it. Why was that so hard?"

Santa closed his eyes and nodded. "It might be easier to show than to explain," he said, then looked at me. "Hello, Charlotte. I wish you had not seen the events here, but I felt it was important."

I opened my mouth to speak, but couldn't decide on which question came first.

"Come and rest," he said, nodding to a bench next to the building. He eased his large frame onto it and sighed. "You have been through a lot today. Both of you."

I took a deep breath and collected my thoughts. "Where are Dr. Friedrich and—"

"They are safe, dear girl," Santa said with a sad smile. "I dropped off some supplies so Otto could repair *Dasher* and he collected the scientist." He held up his wrist to look at an old timepiece. "I programmed a destination into the ship's navigation log to collect you two as well, but we needed to speak first."

I felt the beginnings of some tears I wanted to fight over learning everyone was okay. It was one thing to get stuck in time myself, but to bring others along... I shook my head, clearing it as the continuing shouts from inside the room fought for my attention. Stepping back, I pointed my thumb behind me toward the window. "What happened here?"

"The Council of Nicaea," Santa said, then sighed. "Are you familiar with the event?"

"Not really. Just that you got into a fight," I said. "I wasn't expecting to see it for myself. What made you so mad you'd hit somebody?"

"That is an excellent question," Santa said, adjusting the cuffs on his long coat. "And one that deserves an answer. Emperor Constantine called three hundred and eighteen bishops of the Christian church from all over to determine the relationship between God and Jesus. Some of us had very strong opinions that were presented...without love."

"Who did you slap?" Mom asked.

"Arius," Santa said, voice tinged with regret. "They brought me before Emperor Constantine, stripped the title of Bishop of Myra from me for a time, and put me in jail."

It was hard imagining Santa behind bars. It surprised me he had wanted to relive this event.

"Why have you been showing us all of this?" I asked.

"Perspective, Miss Charlotte," Santa said. "I find it important to remember how things came to be, and how we may change...but throughout time, we still have every version of ourselves living inside. You and I are lucky enough to be able to revisit them."

"So far, it's older versions of myself finding me," I said, thinking back to the Alicorn and wondering what would drive me to become her in the future.

Santa nodded. "Yes, well, you are new to this journey," he said. "Remember that every time you encounter yourself, it is just you revisiting your past. Sometimes there is a benefit to returning to more innocent days."

"This is an innocent day?" I asked, half regretting it.

He offered a merciful smile. "Miss Charlotte, this tour is as much for you as it is for me," he said. "An opportunity to learn and understand for the both of us. For me, I was arguing the case of ultimate love and sacrifice, but had done so while letting my emotion get the better of me." He bowed his head. "It is a lesson I have taken to heart since, to better consider others with my words...and actions."

"So you gave gifts to the rest of the world to make up for it?" I asked. "Seems like a pretty enormous commitment."

Santa chuckled, a glimmer of the familiar laugh peeking through. "I did not do that to make up for what I did here, but to imitate what was modeled for me to copy."

The building's front door burst open and the crowd spilled out, bringing the soon-to-be-former Bishop Nicholas of Myra to his sentencing. Everyone was so caught up in the mob mentality that nobody noticed us.

"But I believe those days may have run their course," Santa said with a deep sigh.

"Yes, about that," Mom said, crossing her arms. "The note on your desk back on the moon said you were making one last trip. Why are you leaving?"

He lifted a bushy, white eyebrow. "Few get to say they visited the moon, you know."

"That doesn't answer the question," I said.

"The right question has not been asked...yet."

"What is the right question?" I was tiring of the riddles. Here I was, face to face with Santa, which should have been a mission accomplished by itself, but there was still so much I didn't understand.

"I wish I could tell you," he said. "If I did, none of this would make any sense."

I closed my eyes tightly until I saw stars behind my eyelids. "I don't get it."

"You will," Santa said. "I promise. But there is another stop ahead, and it will be a long journey."

## Fifteen

NICHOLAS PRESSED A BUTTON ON HIS METAL BELT
buckle, which looked quite similar to Otto's, and a
fine green tendril of light escaped as though he were
releasing the northern lights.

A static wash of pops and crackles filled my ears
as the light grew. Tingles ran from head to toe and
my hair started to stand on end.

Reaching out a gloved hand to both Mom and me,
Santa said, "Hold on tight."

The moment our hands met, brightness enveloped
us completely and the ground beneath our feet disappeared. It felt like I was both soaring and falling
at the same time.

The dials on Santa's watch spun madly. If I had to
guess, it was how he could tell when he was heading.

Odd sounds roared by, playing through the history flying by.

"Where are we going?" I shouted.

Santa looked down at me and smiled. "To give you the rest of the story—"

Before he could finish, we landed firmly on something, and my knees buckled as I lost my grasp on Santa's hand.

The static and light washed away, but my eyes had gotten so used to the brightness that I had to squint to let my vision catch up with what I was hearing.

People were chattering, lots of footsteps all around...and *Christmas music*?

Chaos surrounded me. It was a mall, but larger than I had ever seen. Crowds bustled about in waves and it was difficult for Mom and me to not fall in with the flow of traffic. I wondered how nobody seemed to care that we had appeared out of thin air, but everyone was busy staring at their devices or wearing some sort of headset that looked like a virtual reality game or something.

Santa wasn't with us. Hopefully, he had just stepped away instead of jumping again to leave us on our own.

"I think we're in the future..." Mom said, taking in the sights.

Digital billboards hung in the air outside every shop, flashing with eye-grabbing animation that spun and changed colors to try to compete with

102

their neighbors for people's attention. It was almost too much of a sensory overload to take in.

"Santa?" I called out, turning my head and avoiding the busy shoppers who were coming close to dragging us into the flow of foot traffic.

"He's over there," one guy said, pointing toward the center of the big open area before he disappeared into the crowd.

Mom and I dipped and dodged to see where he had pointed.

Up on a large stage was a red throne and a line of kids and parents ready to take pictures with the man himself.

"How did he get all the way over there?" I said, then realized this was likely one of his employees... but the similarity was too close to not be him.

I pushed farther away from the crowd and put my back to a toy store so I could stand on my tiptoes for a better view.

A boy who looked to be about Petals' age stepped up to the throne with an encouraging nudge from his mother. He gave an uncertain glance at the hovering drone that I guess had replaced the photographer in whatever year this was.

As he moved to sit down on Santa's lap, his mother rushed to him. Santa fuzzed from reality and the boy disappeared completely, except for his little legs sticking out of what was just a hologram of Santa.

The kid started to cry, and his mother consoled him and pulled him out of the chair and stood him next to the fake Santa.

"So, if that isn't him, where is he?" Mom said.

A loud pop from behind caused us both to startle. It was bad enough that my eyes and ears felt like they were going crazy with all the lights and noises.

"Sorry, miss," a familiar voice said.

I brought my gaze down to the little robot, who stood about half of my height.

"Espee!" I said, dropping to a knee. "How did you get here?"

"I work here!" Espee said, holding a bundle of balloons tied to strings in his right hand. He pulled a yellow one loose and offered it to me. "Please have a free balloon, courtesy of Hank's Toy Emporium! Do come inside to check out our fine selection of wooden trains and other sustainable products. Also, may I ask…who is Espee?"

"Espee," I repeated. "That's your name."

"I do not have a name," he said cheerfully. "Mr. Hank did not think it necessary to give me one, I—" A balloon inflated from his mouth too quickly and popped, causing me to fall back into Mom.

"Another?" A man wearing a brown apron with the name Hank embroidered onto it stepped out. "You're busting more than you're making. I'll have to send you in for repairs."

"I regret to inform you that I am two days out of warranty," Espee said. "Did you happen to buy the extended—"

"No! Those are garbage," Hank said, grabbing the rest of the balloons from Espee. "And so are you. No point in having you if you can't hand these things out to convince people to come inside and buy something from me. Go put yourself in the dumpster out back and switch off."

"Whoa," I said, stepping between Hank and Espee. "You're throwing him away?"

"I'm too busy to do that," Hank said. "And I don't have the patience to scrap him, either. Maybe the dump can use him."

"You can't," I said. "That's not right."

"What's not right is how much he cost and how little I got out of him," Hank said.

"What would you like for the robot?" a man said behind me. I knew that voice too.

"Sa...Nicholas?" I said, turning around. A version of Santa—not as old as the one I had traveled here with, and wearing plain, brown clothes—stood in front of me. He glanced down at me.

He cocked his head to the side. "Charlotte, the girl who does not age," he said. "It has been a while. I assume the stocking delivery was successful?"

"Two grand," Hank said, waving his hand at Santa to get his attention. "He's a collector's item."

105

"You were going to throw him away," I said.

"You are bad for business, is what you are," Hank said, angrily pointing a finger at me. "Two-and-a-half grand."

"I do not think that is how negotiations work," Nicholas said.

Hank eyed me, then Nicholas. "Whatever. I just never want to see him again, got it?" He stormed back into the store.

"Thank you," Espee said quietly, looking down at his little robot feet.

"Of course," Nicholas said. "And I have the perfect job for you, if you would like to have it."

"Does it involve balloons?" Espee asked.

"Only if you want it to," Nicholas said with a smile.

"Hey," I said, tapping on Nicholas' arm. "You wouldn't have seen...*yourself*, by any chance, would you?"

"Only every time I look in the mirror," Nicholas said, then drew his lips into a thin line. "But I suspect I understand the notion of what you are after. It is not 'me' me you're looking for, is it? And it is certainly not that imposter over there." He pointed at the fake Santa on the throne.

I shook my head.

"I will make you a deal," Santa said. "Assuming this is a forthcoming version of me, seeing as I do not remember this conversation before, future me will hang back and find you right after this is over. Sound good?"

"I…think so?" I said.

"Excellent," Nicholas said. "Now, come, little one, it is time for a lunar adventure."

Espee lifted a hand for Santa to take and waved at me with his other arm.

I watched the two of them walk away and a mitten fell on my shoulder and patted it twice. For a moment, I wondered why Espee didn't recognize me when we met, but then I remembered he said he'd had a partial memory wipe.

I took a breath, counted down from three, then turned on my heel. The older, more tired version of Nicholas we had traveled here with stood behind me. "I was wondering where you had gone."

"Yes, I had some last-minute shopping to get done," he said with a wry grin.

"So that was where you found Espee," Mom said, nodding toward the little robot trailing off in the distance, getting lost in the crowd.

"Espee?"

"We gave him a name," I said. "He said he liked soda pop. S. P. …Espee."

"Ah. Well, I was glad to save him from the dumpster," Nicholas said, then gestured to the surrounding mall. "Too much gets thrown away."

"Why did you bring us here?"

"This is when two things happened," Santa said. "One, I came to this time to buy all the machinery you saw on the moon to keep up with the production of Christmas assembly lines."

"Why did you do that?" I asked.

Nicholas shrugged. "My original helpers made the toys…which was fine when they carved rocking horses and knit doll dresses, but the times outpaced them. Plus, I did not want them to be apart from their families with the growing demand. I decided they would become my eyes and ears around the world. The machines did the work and saved us all some time."

"That's nice of you," I said, nodding. "What was the second thing?"

"I saw this," Santa said, waving an arm at the mall. "And it made me very, very sad."

"Sad enough to want to quit being Santa?"

"Yes." Nicholas took a deep breath and let it out slowly, then gave me a kind smile. "This was the beginning of the end."

## Sixteen

"The end?" I said, my voice louder than I meant for it to be. People in the crowd took notice of us. "You can't go away. I mean, everybody retires after a while, but...*Christmas.*"

"Christmas is not what it used to be, Charlotte," Nicholas said with a sigh. "I am partially to blame, if I am being honest with myself. Look over there at the hologram. I am not needed."

I shook my head. "That's not better than a real person. What will kids think?" I asked, Petals and Roger coming to mind. "Some don't believe in you, but what would they say if they found out you quit?"

Nicholas shrugged. "I am a symbol now," he said. "And one I wished stood for love instead of cueing minds across the world that it is just time to get presents."

"So why did you want us to see all of this?" Mom asked, pointing to the crowded plaza. "Why are we on this journey?"

"I…" Nicholas began, then sighed. "I wanted someone to understand why I needed to retire. I fear I have pulled the focus away from the love that this season represents."

Mom cocked her head to the side. "That seems like a bit of a stretch," she said, gesturing to the people bustling about us. "They could be buying things for the people they love."

Nicholas nodded. "And I am certain many of them are. For some, Christmas is a time to remember to think of others. But often a gift is given with the expectation of receiving something in return. Granted, not all are given like that, but I fear too many are."

For a moment, I remembered my wish list and how I had barely put any thought to what I would give to the rest of my family. I had been putting myself first.

"If you wait to show love to someone until they show love to you," Nicholas said. "Then the entire world will wait…and grow bitter. And angry."

"So, how do we go back?" I asked. "What would make you want to continue being Santa? You have a lot of influence. People would listen to you."

Nicholas shook his head. "If I showed up and spoke to everyone," he said, "nobody would believe it. We need to show love in the small, meaningful ways that we can. Helping others. Even if it is just one person at a time…" He held up a finger. "And it

110

has to be done *without* the expectation of something in return."

"Like the three daughters," I said. "They couldn't pay you back and didn't know who to thank."

"Not every gift has to involve money." He glanced at his watch. "No matter what they say, time is not money. Money is not time. Time is far more valuable than that. You can always earn more money, but once time is spent, it is gone. Even with us, being able to hop around it and getting to live it out of order, we have a finite amount of time to make a difference for good."

"Where are you going to go?" I asked, the sting of tears forming in the corners of my eyes. "This doesn't feel right."

"I might visit some old friends," Nicholas said. "Perhaps deliver the odd present here and there. Thank you for taking the time to find me, Charlotte. It is good to know that someone was concerned and not just looking to get on the nice list."

A thought came to mind. It was awful timing, but this was my only chance.

"Can I make a request? Before you retire?"

Nicholas gave half a frown and crossed his arms. He gestured around himself. "There is no workshop here. I have no tools. I fear you missed my point."

"No, no, I don't want a present," I said, then lowered my voice to a whisper. "Well, I do, but not one for me."

Nicholas nodded as though he knew where I was going with this. He glanced over my shoulder at Mom. "I am sorry," he said. "I promise I looked into it. Even tried to help. But I was stopped."

"By who?" I asked.

"You," Nicholas said, then sighed. "Come, there is something I would very much like for you to see before we go on and try to play with history."

*I* messed up Mom's Christmas request? That didn't seem fair. All I could think about was the scared little girl at the mall with the teddy bear arm ripped off. "What did I do?"

"You did nothing wrong, Charlotte," Nicholas said. "You were protecting me. Come and see."

Nicholas had Mom and me follow him to a wing of the mall with several closed down stores, then offered his hands.

"We must take care when light jumping," he said. "Too many witnesses will attract the wrong sort of attention."

I lifted my eyebrow. "You mean like if someone reports a time traveling Santa, then the S.o.T.T. could show up?"

"Not exactly," Nicholas said. "But very close."

Once more, the belt buckle engaged and light enveloped us. I wasn't sure if the feeling of flying and falling at the same time would be something I would ever get used to.

Thankfully, before I knew it, we were back on solid ground, standing on a sidewalk in an average-looking neighborhood. Something crackled like static behind me, and I turned to see a house covered by a dome of shimmering, buzzing electricity.

I cautiously extended a hand out at the crackling force field ahead of me, but before my fingers could reach it, I was yanked backward.

"Please do not touch that," Nicholas said, steadying me and giving me a reassuring pat on my shoulder. "Very dangerous."

"Wait a moment," Mom said, peering through the haze. "I know this place." She put a hand over her mouth. "This is where I grew up."

"It certainly is," Nicholas said. "And as you can see, I could not get in."

"What is this dome thing?" I asked, wishing I hadn't let curiosity get the better of me.

"Let us have her explain it," Nicholas said, pointing along the bright wall.

One yard over, someone wearing a hooded jacket stood with her arms folded, talking to another, younger version of Nicholas.

With a flash of light, he was gone. The hooded lady walked over at a fast pace.

"Hold on," I said. "You said I kept you from… taking care of things."

The figure removed the hood, revealing—

"Charlotte?" Mom asked.

"Lottie," I said at the same time as the teenage version of myself.

"We have to stop meeting like this," Lottie said with a smirk. "And we can't stick around here for too long. The Order has eyes and ears everywhere."

"The who?" I asked.

Lottie rubbed her temples. "It would break my brain to learn this from myself. Nick, could you please explain to her what I just explained to you over there?"

"That was years ago for me," Nicholas said. "But if memory serves, The Order is a group of people inside the Society of Time Travelers who are trying to...control things."

"That's...putting it lightly," Lottie said. "Hi, Mom. Good to see you."

"Hi, honey...can someone explain why my child-hood home has been blocked by a giant dome that isn't safe to touch?"

"Hold on," I said, waving my arms. "I can't trust the S.o.T.T.? But don't I become like...important there or something?"

"I can't tell you," Lottie said. "Because when I was standing where you were, future me didn't tell me. Just...you need to be careful, and I promise you'll figure it out." She turned to Mom. "And, yes, for a reason I can't explain right now, I had to warn Santa

114

from trying to get in through The Order's dome, which meant Grandma couldn't come home for Christmas. I know that's been kind of a sore spot for you, but it's not the big guy's fault." She narrowed her eyes at Santa. "I mean, assuming you're not in charge of The Order."

Nicholas gave a deep laugh. "I am not, and I wish this was the only time I have run into them before," he said. "But there are ways to work around this."

"Oh, now you're coming to the fun part," Lottie said, turning on her heel and walking away down the sidewalk. "I'll leave you all to it."

"Wait, does the fun part mean more falling?" I called after my older self.

"You'll see!" Lottie said, waving an arm without looking back. She pulled a Chrono from her belt and aimed it at the air in front of her. With a blast, a blue portal formed, and she stepped through.

"Does that happen often?" Mom asked. "Seeing yourself, I mean."

"Not the first time, and since I'll see this again eventually from her side, it won't be the last," I said. "What did I...*she* mean? Where are we going next?"

"To make a delivery," Nicholas said as he reached down to activate the device in his belt buckle. "Hold tight."

Lights flashed, and the world transformed again.

115

The light gave way to an almost as bright field of snow next to a crystal blue lake with a sea plane sitting by its shore.

"No..." Mom said, walking over to get a better look.

"Did we land where we were supposed to?" I asked. "What is it?"

"That's my mother's plane."

## SEVENTEEN

"THANK YOU!" I SHOUTED, LOOKING FOR NICHOLAS to give him a big hug. But with a blast of light, he was gone. Why didn't he stick around?

"Wait, you did this?" Mom asked.

I nodded, wearing a massive grin. "It's your present," I said. "You wanted to spend Christmas with your mom." We stood at the edge of a forest, and Mom immediately stepped behind a large tree.

Off in the distance, storm clouds skittered with lightning. Thunder followed, barely masked by the churning of the water plane's running engine. There was no way my grandmother could hear us.

"Charlotte, wait," Mom said, grabbing my sleeve. "Please."

I stopped in my tracks and turned to face her. "What's wrong?"

"I wasn't ready for something like this," Mom said, dabbing at the corner of her eye. "Time travel is a lot to drop on someone." She pointed at the plane in the distance. "Your grandma is my age right now. Why would she believe that I'm her daughter?"

The first patter of rain fell on my head as storm clouds blew in above.

"But if we could convince her…" I began. "Wouldn't it be nice to show her you turned out okay? Maybe give her some peace?"

In a forest clearing behind us, *Dasher* appeared. Nicholas must have given them the location to meet here. The ramp lowered and Dr. Friedrich, Otto, and Espee walked out.

"Oh, Canada," Dr. Friedrich said, stepping up next to Mom, shivering. "A bit cold for my liking. Would anyone care to inform me why we're here on Christmas Eve?"

"My mom didn't make it home for Christmas when I was little," Mom said, "so Charlotte asked Nicholas to bring me here for the reunion."

"I see," Dr. Friedrich said with a solemn nod. "Charlotte, this is a heavy thing for a parent. And we must remember that what happened, happened."

"Well, The Order is keeping us from getting her home on time, so maybe the next best thing is spending Christmas with her grown-up daughter?" I said. "We're always finding loopholes like these."

"The Order is involved?" Dr. Friedrich asked, eyes widening. "This is growing more and more complicated, Charlotte."

In the distance, my grandmother exited the plane wearing a yellow rain jacket, making her stand out against the dark horizon. She loaded up the last box from the shore.

"She needs to wait out this storm," Otto said, placing a hand over his forehead as the rain started falling harder around us. "Flying into something like that isn't safe at all."

My eye caught a blur of motion as the loading ramp lifted and closed. Soon, the propeller spun to a blur.

"Maybe she was thinking getting home for Christmas was more important than being safe," I said, looking at Mom. My shoulders slumped. I had gotten so close to reuniting them, and now the chance was slipping away.

The plane puttered out from the shore. Above, the sky let loose with a rush of rain, completely soaking me and everyone standing on *Dasher*'s ramp.

"We need to make sure she doesn't crash," I said, turning around and running up the ramp.

"But she won't crash," Mom said, wiping the rain from her face now that we were out of the storm. "She'll make it home after Christmas. And you said that whatever happened, happened, right?"

I had to think about that for a moment. "But if lightning hits her plane, and it goes down, we might be the ones to save her."

"We also might not," Mom said. "If we just left, something else would save her."

I couldn't tell if Mom just wanted to avoid seeing Grandma. I didn't want to give up on Mom getting her chance to see her own mother again. "But we're here, and we can help keep her safe if she needs it."

Mom nodded and gave a slight smile as the rain ran down her face. She knelt down and grabbed me in a tight hug. "I'm proud of you, Charlotte."

"Strap in, everyone," Otto said from the pilot's seat. He flipped three toggles to bring the engines to life. "We're not going to have much easier of a time than she will in wind and rain like this. One lightning strike and…" He made a crashing noise with his mouth that I didn't care for. "Oh no…"

"What?" I asked, buckling into the seat next to Otto.

"Cloaking is still busted," Otto said. "*Dasher* must have lost it when the flare hit us. We won't be able to hide from her."

The sea plane got itself up to speed and took off from the lake. It wobbled back and forth as gusty winds rocked it.

*Dasher* lifted, its engines whining and bucking against the storm. Rain pounded on the view screen.

"Mind pressing that blue button with the picture of a water drop over there?" Otto asked, pointing to the console in front of me.

120

Searching for the button among dozens of others, I finally located and pressed it. Windshield wipers started swinging to clear our vision.

"Appreciate it," Otto said, continuing to pull back on the controls, pinning us all to our seats.

"I didn't realize I was in the co-pilot chair," I said, mindful to not lean forward and accidentally press any of the other buttons.

"How about we keep a safe distance?" Dr. Friedrich said. "If she sees time travel technology, we don't want her to panic.

Otto lowered *Dasher* into my grandmother's blind spot behind her.

All around, a fog lifted from the waters, easily hiding us, but also making it more difficult for Otto.

A bolt of lightning came down from the sky, striking *Dasher*. I screamed as sparks shot out of the console and smoke spilled out, causing us to cough and choke.

"Stand back!" Espee said, stepping forward with a fire extinguisher.

I couldn't get out of my restraints to avoid the white, foamy material that was almost as bad as the smoke, but at least there wasn't a fire growing right in front of me.

"Systems are trying to repair themselves," Otto shouted, using one hand to wave to clear the air in front of his face. "But we have to gain altitude."

We rose out of the fog and into the skies, once more spotting my grandmother's sea plane.

Just in time to watch it get struck by lightning.

The sea plane's right engine caught on fire, black smoke billowing out and mixing with the rain. Flames peeked out just behind the propeller.

"We have to save her!" I shouted. "Otto, can you get closer?"

"I'm trying to keep *us* from crashing!"

Swiveling in my chair, I turned to face Dr. Friedrich. "Could you call someone with your Chrono? Have the S.o.T.T. prepared to catch us?"

Dr. Friedrich shook his head. "At this point in my timeline, I am *persona non grata* there."

"What language is that?"

"Latin," Dr. Friedrich said, stiffening his posture. "It means I'm not exactly welcome there anymore."

"What?" I shouted. "Why?"

"The Order. But let's make sure we live through this first," Dr. Friedrich said. "I am afraid we are her best chance."

Otto brought *Dasher* up closer to my grandmother's prop plane, although our own engine coughed and sputtered. We briefly dropped once, sending my stomach lurching into my chest. Getting her to jump over to our ship wasn't a much better situation, but at least we weren't on fire.

"*Dasher* to Sea Plane, *Dasher* to Sea Plane, come in,

Sea Plane, you're damaged," Otto said over the ship's comm. "We're here to help."

No response.

"Her radio might be fried," Otto said.

I felt a hand reach up onto my shoulder and give me a squeeze. "It'll be okay, sweetheart," Mom said, although the tone of her voice wasn't reassuring.

My grandmother spotted us as we leveled off beside her. Her eyes shot open wide, and she immediately steered her plane away.

To be fair, I didn't blame her. To her, our ship probably looked like it was an alien or something.

"I'm sorry," I said back to Mom.

"For what?"

"This is—" The ship shook uncontrollably for a moment. I grasped the arms of the chair so tightly I imagined the metal was going to bend. "—the worst Christmas present ever."

"She's climbing!" Otto said, pointing as the prop plane disappeared into the storm clouds above. "Why doesn't she land on the water?"

"She probably thinks we're chasing her," I said.

"A pilot can get really turned around in the clouds," Otto said.

"What if we take her to another time?" Espee asked.

"Do what?" I asked.

"This is a time travel machine," he said. "But if you

123

get close enough to something else, you can bring it with you."

"A solar stasis field!" Dr. Friedrich cried out, smacking his forehead with his palm. "Of course!"

"When would we even take her?" I asked.

"Let me check," Otto said, pressing some buttons. "Wait. The destination time has been pre-programmed already. I can't change it."

"Who would have done that—" I started, then I spotted it. Through the haze inside the ship, a monitor half-covered in fire extinguisher spray showed that Nicholas had not just locked in one destination on the computer, but many. "Nicholas."

"Probably because he didn't trust me to not bring this technology to the S.o.T.T.," Dr. Friedrich said in a huff. "Naughty list, indeed."

"He wants us to go somewhere else," I said, looking at the latitude and longitude coordinates.

"Wait, the solar stasis field needs a target to lock onto inside her plane," Otto said. "Something of Santa's."

Wheels turned in my head. "You have the candle, right?" I said, pointing to Dr. Friedrich.

"Um, yes…" Dr. Friedrich said, pulling the lump of wax from his pocket and handing it to me.

"But she isn't responding to the radio," Espee said. "How would she know what we're trying to do?"

"I'll tell her," I said with a smile.

"How?" Mom asked.

"Otto, I need to borrow your time looper," I said.

Otto smacked his head with his palm, then quickly grabbed *Dasher*'s controls again. "I see where you're going with this. But, wait, that would put you on a crashing plane."

"No way," Mom said.

"I think it's the only way," I said, pointing to the plane's window. I checked my watch to note the time and remember this moment, then looked up. "See?"

Another version of me waved back through the sea plane's window.

# Eighteen

"Otto, your time loop belt," I said. "I need it to jump to before we took off."

He struggled with removing the buckle and handed it to me. "Hold on tight," he said. "Swipe the dial to how far you want to go back and slam the button."

"Got it," I said, guessing at how long ago we had landed on the shore as I turned the knob back and set a timer on my watch to match it.

"Now, it won't take you to the exact place—"

I pressed the button, engaging the light loop, and immediately fell for half a second as the ground rushed up to meet me.

The wind pushed out from my lungs and I rolled on the hard dirt until my stomach met an enormous tree trunk.

Sucking in air, I pulled myself up to see my grandma's sea plane idling on the water just off the shore.

I was back where we first arrived. Deeper into the forest sat *Dasher*.

Flexing my shoulder as I stood made me wince, but I took off toward the beach.

I had to think through what I could and couldn't do and how I would need to time everything. Regardless of what I was going to do, my grandma took off, so there would be no convincing her not to fly.

The entire purpose of me being a stowaway was to make the connection to light jump her to safety, so she didn't even have to know I was onboard.

Once more, I watched her carrying the boxes of supplies by herself up the back ramp. I wouldn't be able to sneak past her without getting caught, so I waited for her to finish her last load, and when she walked in and sat in the pilot's seat, I bolted down the beach.

The whirring of the door being pulled shut caused me to run even faster, and thankfully, with the sound of the propellers starting up, she couldn't hear me huffing and puffing as I jumped inside before the back gate closed with a loud clang.

"This is India Bravo, Niner-Niner," Grandma said into the headset she wore over her curly hair. "See you on the next rebound. Over."

"I still say this is a terrible idea," a man's voice said over the comm unit. "You won't beat that storm. Stay another day at camp to let this blow over...over."

"Negative," Grandma said, flipping three switches and checking gauges. "I promised my daughter I'd make it back for Christmas. Over."

"Well, if the weather takes you out, there won't be any more promi—"

Grandma flicked off the communication unit before base camp could keep trying to convince her how bad an idea it was to take off.

*So that's why we couldn't reach her over the radio,* I thought as I hid behind a large box. I wished there was a seat or some way to strap myself in because I knew I'd be in for a bumpy ride.

The roar of the engines shook the plane as we lurched forward, and I slid to the back of the cargo area.

The nose of the plane lifted, and we were airborne. A loud scraping noise alerted me to the giant wooden crate sliding toward me.

My eyes shot open. I dove to the side, narrowly avoiding being pinned to the wall by the box that was several times my size.

Grandma must have been in a serious rush to leave if she hadn't tied everything down.

I caught my breath and checked my watch. We weren't too far from when things were about to go downhill, so I hugged my knees to my chest and grabbed onto some safety netting.

"What on earth?" Grandma shouted, looking out the side window. "What kind of plane is *that*?"

Lightning flashed outside, followed immediately by a deafening crack of thunder that caused Grandma to jerk the controls to the side. The roar of fire joined in as black smoke began belching out of the plane's engine.

I screamed, then covered my mouth. Grandma turned her head and made eye contact with me.

She screamed.

I screamed again.

The plane dove.

"Wait, wait, wait!" I said, trying to run toward the cockpit, but my feet left the floor...until she yanked back on the flight stick and I fell flat on my face.

"Ow..."

"What? Who? This is not okay!" Grandma shouted. "Wait...Renee?"

I pulled myself up slowly and shook my head. "Please," I said. "Just try to fly close to that other plane."

"You mean alien," Grandma said.

"It's not..." I had to take in a deep breath. "...an alien. *Please*. I'm trying to save you so you can see your daughter at Christmas."

"We're on *fire!*" Grandma's jaw dropped. "I...I'm losing my mind, aren't I?"

"Uh...no." My watch timer beeped. "But hold that thought," I said. It was time. Out the window next to me, I gave a short wave to myself, then pulled the wax from my pocket and pressed it against the window.

A green beam of light shot out from *Dasher* and connected to the lump of candle wax, then wrapped itself around the plane.

"Watch out!" Grandma shouted as the view out the windshield changed from a stormy sky to dancing red tendrils of light.

I shook my head. *How did we get back to Iceland?*

But before I could give it much thought, a pulse of green shot out and we jumped right to clear blue skies.

Beneath it was the island with the S.o.T.T. head-quarters! Were we being brought in for a crash water landing?

Another flash. Another location change. The reindeer bay on Santa's base.

The silver surroundings went by in a blur as the plane landed hard and screeched to a halt, throwing me back down to the floor.

A long moment passed.

"Are you all right back there?" Grandma called out as she unbuckled herself and rushed over to help me.

"I think I need to just roll myself in bubble wrap before going on these trips," I said, choosing to lie on the cold metal until she offered me a hand up.

Outside, the hiss of fire extinguishers filled the air. They must have been putting out the engine flames.

"Charlotte!" Mom's voice called from outside. "Are you okay?"

Grandma stepped over broken crates to work the controls that lowered the back ramp.

Small robots hosed down both *Dasher* and Grandma's sea plane and left a dense white fog everywhere that mixed with dark smoke.

Mom ran over to us from across the hangar.

"What is going on?" Grandma said, waving her hand in front of her face. She froze the moment she saw Mom. "Is that...are you...am I...*Renee*?"

Mom nodded, wiping a tear away. "Hi, Mom," she said. "I know it's a lot to process,"

I looked at the two women, their faces almost identical. They had the same blue eyes and the button nose Petals had inherited. My grandmother had darker skin and more freckles, probably from all the time she spent outside doing her animal research. The two could have been sisters.

"Did I miss it?" Grandma asked.

"Miss what?" Mom said, not stepping forward.

Grandma motioned around with her hands. "Everything," she said. "Did I die?"

I didn't exactly want to overwhelm her with an explanation, but my grandmother needed to have at least some idea of what was going on. "You're..." I began. "We're on the moon. Santa must have thought it would be the safest place to land."

Grandma understandably gave me the most confused face I've ever seen on a person. Then her knees buckled.

Mom moved in to hold her up. "Easy, Mom, easy," she said, then turned to me. "We have to take this slowly."

"I was trying to get home in time for Christmas," Grandma said. "But you saved me…a version of you from the future saved me?" Her eyes locked on me. "And is this your daughter?"

I nodded. "One of them."

A loud warning alarm blared throughout the hangar, forcing us all to cover our ears. The bay doors above opened out to space and a sleek, sleigh-like ship lowered slowly through a crackling magnetic field and onto a landing pad.

The hatch on top of the sleigh opened, and out climbed Santa Claus, wearing the traditional red suit with white fur trim. He let out a loud sigh as he looked us all over.

"Ho-ho-what have we here?"

## Nineteen

"Hello," I said cautiously.

"Oh, Charlotte," Santa said. "You never cease to surprise. And...Otto? What are you doing here?"

Otto pointed at the wrecked water plane in the hangar, which made Santa jump back. "It's going to take some explaining."

"Santa!" Espee exclaimed, toddling off the ship's ramp.

"And who is this?" Santa asked, furrowing his brow.

Espee stopped in his tracks, then bowed his head. "I guess we haven't met yet. My future Santa is still out there somewhere."

"Is that...really Santa?" Grandma asked, leaning in close to Mom.

"One of many names," Nicholas said with a tired smile. "It is a pleasure to meet you, Margaret."

"I'd ask how you know my name," Grandma said, "but I guess that's kind of your thing."

Santa nodded. "It is." He turned to Mom. "So, let me get this straight. You, Renee, when you were about your daughter's current age, asked for your mother to make it home for Christmas."

"I did," Mom said with a sad smile.

"So, mission accomplished...a couple of decades after the fact," Santa said, pulling off his mittens. "I do apologize for the delay, but it was out of my hands." He took a deep breath and let it out slowly, his shoulders slumping. "I am afraid I really must excuse myself. These sorts of runs take it out of me nowadays, and I am due for a good, deep sleep."

"I'm sorry," I said, stepping forward. "And thank you." I reached my arms out for a hug, and Nicholas matched the motion for a hug. "All of this has been a miracle," I said, my voice muffled in the fluffy white lining of his suit.

I stepped back and pulled out a small notebook and pen from my pocket. "One last thing. When you've decided it's time to retire...could you promise to meet me here?" I jotted down a time and place and ripped off the page. "Before it's *goodbye*, goodbye."

Santa accepted the paper, glanced at it, then tucked it into his coat with a tired smile. "I will be there, Miss Charlotte."

"Merry Christmas," I said.

"Merry Christmas," Santa replied as he walked out of the hangar and toward his quarters.

"What was that?" Mom said.

"You'll see," I said with a smile. "But maybe first we should give Grandma a tour."

"Of the moon?" Grandma asked.

"Not quite," I said. "Otto, can I please ask for another quick trip with zero explosions or fires or getting lost in time?"

Otto chuckled. "I kind of wish you had asked for that in the first place."

I walked up the ramp of the new ship, then turned to find Espee still frozen. "Hey, come on, we're not done yet."

The little robot perked up and followed us into *Dancer*, the less banged up brother to *Dasher*. It was as though the ship had been reset and we had the chance for a do-over.

As we all buckled in, I looked over at my grandma and realized how little I knew about her beyond her name being Margaret and that she had gone on adventures that took her away from my mother for long periods of time. While I could never dream of telling her about the future, I had to assume she would figure out on her own that she had passed before I was born.

Otto pressed the right series of buttons and motioned for me to input the date for when we

135

should travel. I turned the dial to a year a couple of decades ahead.

"That won't get me home for your Christmas," Grandma said.

Mom looked at me, then the date, and mouthed, 'thank you.'

"Cloaking on," Otto said, flipping a switch. "Glad that's working on this ship. Have to make sure nobody spots us, right?"

The world shifted to the neighborhood I had spent the first nine years of my life in.

It was summer, and the trees and grass were green. I got up and pressed the button by the door, opening it.

We had traveled to when I was three days old. It was when Mom was bringing her first child back to the safety of her home.

"Dr. Friedrich," I said. "Can my grandma borrow your necklace so nobody recognizes her?"

"Of course, my dear," Dr. Friedrich said, slipping the device out from beneath his collar and handing it to a very confused Grandma.

"What does this do?" Grandma asked.

"Not make things awkward," I said.

Dr. Friedrich gave a shooing motion with his hands. "We'll stay here and give you some privacy."

Mom, Grandma, and I hurried out of *Dancer* just in time for my family's old van...well, currently *new* van, Oliver rounded the corner and pulled into the driveway.

My mother, in her twenties, eased out of the passenger side as Dad ran over to help her stand.

We approached on the opposite sidewalk, looking completely different from ourselves. Neither young Mom nor Dad noticed us as they focused on the little bundle in the car seat one row back.

Three-day-old Charlotte had pulled the pink beanie the hospital had given her down over her eyes, but wasn't fussing.

"Let me help you with that," the younger version of my mom said, tugging up on the cap to release a shocking amount of dark brown hair. She leaned in and kissed the newborn softly on the forehead, waking her.

A soft cry traveled on the wind as young Mom unbuckled baby Charlotte and gently lifted her newborn to her shoulder.

"You were so small," Mom whispered, squeezing my hand. "I was afraid I would break you."

"You learn kids are a lot tougher than you think," Grandma said, her voice thick with emotion. "I can't believe I'm seeing this."

The family made it through the front door, successful in bringing their firstborn home from the hospital.

Grandma wiped at her eyes with her sleeve, turning away. "I hate to ask," she said, "but why am I not here for this?"

A long pause hung in the air. Tears welled in the corner of Mom's eyes, which said enough.

"I…I understand," Grandma said.

"You were here," Mom said, putting a hand over her heart, then patting it. "You've been here for everything."

Grandma nodded. "Thank you…but it's not the same."

"It isn't," Mom said, hugging her mother. "But I'm glad you at least got to see this."

"What if it could be more?" I asked. Both women looked at me. "What if, Grandma, you visited some memories from the outside, like this, but also we pick you up and take some trips with us into the future…"

"That…that would be lovely," Grandma said.

"And Mom, since Grandma went on so many adventures…what if you traveled back in time and joined her on some of them?" I asked. "You might have missed them when you were little, but not this time."

"That would be a pretty big secret to keep," Grandma said, looking at Mom. "But worth it."

Mom smiled and gave Grandma another tight hug. "Come here," she said, waving me in and adding me to the group embrace.

"You've raised a smart girl, Renee," Grandma said. "I'm proud of you. But not just for that."

"Love you, Mom," Mom said.

"Love you too, peanut."

"I know you didn't get home for the Christmas when I was ten," Mom said, "but would you like to spend one with us? You could meet Daisy and Roger too."

Grandma nodded. "I would like nothing more."

# Twenty

I leaned against the island in Dr. Friedrich's kitchen as the decorations and furniture shifted through different styles.

"Ah, there we are," Dr. Friedrich said, turning a knob on his Chrono remote once more. A beach house interior complete with soft ukulele music surrounded us. Mom and Grandma sat in the living room, so deep in catching up with each other that they weren't paying attention to the crazy technological display.

Espee stood on his little robot tiptoes, trying to get a better look out the front window.

"You look like you're going to a beach, not Iceland," I said as Dr. Friedrich walked over to join me in the kitchen.

"Because I am!" he said with a broad smile. "Once I drop you all off for your Christmas, I'll be enjoying some warmer weather on a small island named…

actually I don't remember its proper name. Susanna would know. She picked it out for me."

Dr. Friedrich took in a deep breath and let out a contented sigh.

"Everything okay?" I asked.

He nodded toward the two women who could pass as sisters, still lost in conversation. "It's wonderful, Charlotte. Absolutely wonderful. You know, when I discovered time travel as a younger man, I gave little thought that reunions like this were possible. All I could imagine were great scientific discoveries and witnessing moments in history...but this, at the end of my career...this is what I am most proud of."

Mom and Grandma shared a laugh, the same laugh, and I couldn't help but smile. Mom had done so much for me, and I was grateful to do something like this for her. I turned to Dr. Friedrich. "So is this it? Will I see you again?"

Dr. Friedrich shrugged. "You're more than welcome to come and visit," he said. "But if it's further adventure you're after, which certainly happens, I might suggest bringing along a younger version of myself."

A bell dinged in the house and a red light glowed above the front door. "Ah, Iceland arrives! Everyone, I may recommend grabbing a coat."

"Me too?" Espee asked.

"If you like," Dr. Friedrich said.

I reached over and gave Dr. Friedrich a hug. "Thank you. For everything."

He returned the embrace. "I'm proud of you, Miss Charlotte," he said. "And I'm grateful we became neighbors. Now, go and do great things...but first, enjoy this gift of spending time with your family."

*   *   *

"YOU LIVE IN ICELAND?" Grandma asked as we stepped out of the light rectangle door from the freshly retired Dr. Friedrich's house.

Ahead, smoke puffed out of the chimney of the small cabin our family had rented overlooking the black sand beach and rocks jutting out from the ocean.

"No," Mom said with a laugh as she opened the front door and was immediately met by a running Petals, who almost bowled her over.

"Mommy!" she shouted as she squeezed tightly. She looked up at Grandma. "Are you Mommy's friend?"

Grandma smiled. "I am. What's your name?"

"Petals," she said. "But I'm starting to like Daisy. People also call me precocious, which sounds close to precious, but it doesn't mean the same. I think it's the extra 'co' in the middle that makes it different— you got me a robot!?"

Espee looked at me and I patted his head. "No, no," I said. "He's a friend who is spending Christmas with us."

"Margaret?" Dad said from inside, then froze at the door. "I...uh...*Renee*? Is that really..." He stepped out onto the front porch wearing a puffy yellow winter coat, which Roger was sleepily cuddled into.

Roger immediately informed everyone he wasn't a fan of the icy wind.

"C'mon in," Dad said, opening his eyes wide at me, then turned to Grandma. "It's good to see you, Margaret. Really good."

Dad handed me Roger so he could give his mother-in-law a giant hug. I brought my little brother back into the warmth.

Inside, the cabin had been decked out for Christmas, complete with a crackling fire and the scent of peppermint cocoa wafting from the stove. Dad was particularly proud of the only holiday drink he liked to make.

"Were there unicorns on this trip too?" Petals asked Espee, pointing a finger out from her forehead. She stopped and gasped, hauling me back a step. "Wait, did Santa ride a unicorn?"

"Not that I saw," I said, glad to hear unexpected things come out of my little sister's mouth again.

"So you *saw* Santa?" Petals asked, putting a hand on each of her cheeks.

"Like, so many versions of him," I said, finding my way to an overstuffed couch and falling into it with Roger.

"Christmas is saved!" Petals said, running as close as she dared to the fire and trying her best to look up the chimney.

"Santa is safe," I said, taking a deep sigh. "Christmas is still Christmas, with or without him delivering presents."

"What?" Petals exclaimed. "But, my freeze ray!"

"Mind if I sit here?" Grandma Margaret asked, nodding to the seat beside me.

I patted the cushion, sending a little dust dancing into the warm light of the fire. "Please."

Grandma sat down. She smelled of engine grease and adventure…which was probably the smoke and fire extinguishers from the moon base.

"I wanted to say thank you," Grandma said. "This has been a big day. I'm not sure what I'm supposed to do with everything I know now," she said, shaking her head. "I mean, we only have so many days…" she trailed off, looked at me, and smiled. "We have to make every day count, don't we? I'm grateful that today is one day I get to have."

"Me too," Mom said, sitting down next to Grandma and offering her a mug of cocoa. "Where do you think we should go first?"

"I have that trip to Turkey planned—"

"Maybe a different one," I suggested, imagining Mom not wanting to revisit where we all got stuck.

"No, no," Mom said. "It's okay. There's something good about reclaiming a difficult time." She reached behind her mother's back and squeezed my shoulder. "Thank you. This was the best present I could have asked for."

Dad eased into the cozy-looking recliner by the fire and sighed contentedly.

A knock came at the front door.

Dad glanced at his watch. "Who would show up this late on Christmas Eve?" He stood and walked over to open the door, revealing a balding man in a brown coat with a large, bushy white beard.

"Did...did someone invite—"

"Santa!" Espee shouted, tottering quickly toward the large man, nearly knocking over Dad. "You came back!"

Nicholas laughed as the robot clung to his leg. "That I did." He looked up to Dad. "May I come in?"

Dad blinked twice and shook his head. "Oh, yes, yes, where are my manners? I'm sorry, it's a lot to process."

"I understand," Nicholas said, patting Dad on the shoulder and walking in with Espee at his side.

"So they found you?" Dad asked. "Listen, about that time when I was fourteen. I thought fire was cool, and—"

Nicholas laughed. "You are off the hook. But I am afraid I did not bring any presents."

"That's not why I wanted you here," I said, jumping up from the couch and holding my hands out in an offer to take his coat. "I imagined you were always so busy trying to make sure that everyone else had a good Christmas that you didn't really get many invitations yourself."

Nicholas eased out of his jacket, making a sly move to wipe at his eyes as he did so.

"And now that you've retired," I said, placing the coat on a nearby rack, "I figured your calendar was open."

"You know what? It absolutely was," Nicholas said. He nodded to the rest of my family, then smiled at my mom and grandma. "And you've come to understand one of the most important parts about Christmas."

"Not freeze rays! That's for sure," Petals said from in front of the fireplace.

"Technically, you are correct, Miss Daisy," Nicholas said. "The most important part about Christmas is not a freeze ray."

"Oh?" Dad asked with a smile. "So, what is it?"

"The hope of reunion," Nicholas said, nodding toward the two women on the couch. "And time well spent with love." He smiled as Dad brought over a mug of cocoa. "Thank you for searching for me. Thank you for this reminder that some people recognize that not everything about this season is about exchanging material things. Time is more precious than we all realize. And it is worth fighting for."

He eased himself into a chair by the window and Espee nodded a thanks to me.

"What will you do now?" I asked.

"First, I will enjoy today," he said. "Then I will enjoy tomorrow. Perhaps with a bit of company, eh, Espee?"

The robot stomped his little feet in joy, and a balloon began filling up from his mouth. I braced myself for the pop, but it stopped at the right inflation level and he quickly tied it in a knot. "Merry Christmas, Charlotte," he said, offering it to me.

"Merry Christmas, Espee," I said, taking the balloon.

Dad eased back into his comfy recliner, just in time for another knock came at the door.

"I don't know why I try to sit down," Dad said. "First my mother-in-law shows up, then Santa Claus. I'm pretty sure if it was an alien I wouldn't even be surp—"

"Not an alien," Dad's voice shouted from outside.

"Well, at least it's someone I can trust," Dad said, opening the door to reveal another version of himself, wearing a black and white Icelandic sweater.

"Hi, me," Dad said. "Wait. Is that my Christmas present?"

The slightly older version of Dad looked down at his chest, then smacked his forehead. "Sorry, didn't even think about that. But, yes. It's super warm! You'll love it, I promise. And you're looking handsome, I have to say."

"Why thank you," Dad said with a slight bow. "You're not too shabby yourself. Okay, this is weird. Are you staying?"

Future Dad shook his head. "No, I wanted to revisit a happy memory and deliver this." He offered a thick white envelope.

"What is that?" I asked.

"Your acceptance letter to the S.o.T.T. academy," Future Dad said. "Congrats, kiddo. You're finally about to start your formal training in the Society of Time Travelers."

"Be careful, Charlotte," Nicholas said from behind me. "Beware The Order."

"Don't worry, Nick," Future Dad said. "We're only going there to help take them down."

"We are?" I asked.

"Together," he said with a smile, looking over everyone in the cozy room decorated for Christmas. "As a family."

# About the Author

C.W. Task is a father/daughter duo who began a tradition of telling stories together on long walks after the spark of youthful imagination discovered an invisible house when everyone else just saw a mailbox on an empty lot.

*The Lost Saint* is C.W.'s third entry into the seven book series of *The Invisible House.*

# Acknowledgments

C.W. Task as a plural person has many folks we would like to thank. We would be remiss if we didn't start off by thanking those in our lives who put so much effort into making Christmas-time special. For us, Sarah Dunlap creates the magic with the intentionality that ensures memories are made and should be absolutely celebrated. She also edited this book, and we're grateful for her thoughtful touch and ensuring that the correct number of commas are used.

The astute reader might notice this book is arriving a bit later than expected, and we're grateful for those readers who have made it this far into the story. These last couple of years have been filled with big life events and changes and it turns out that usually you want to release a Christmas-themed book around Christmas… and that's also a very busy time of the year.

The deadline may have been missed *(2.5 times...)*, but thanks to the magic of time travel, you might just be reading it at the exact right time.

We're grateful for those who have gone before us and given and sacrificed so much so we could have the childhoods we did.

And once more, you. Thank you for going on this adventure with Charlotte. The series is at a turning point, and we can't wait for you to explore more in this world with us.

## Fictionsmith Family

Since our family has made a habit of spending time together to tell stories, we started something called Fictionsmith Family! We're aiming to share our process with other families who may be interested in telling stories together.

Join us by heading to FictionsmithFamily.com, and follow us on Instagram, Facebook, and Threads at @FictionsmithFamily for videos, ideas, and more!

Charlotte Jones will return in
*The Infinite Hallway.*